SECRET DESIRE

JILL SANDERS

To my sisters...

DIGITAL ISBN: 978-1-945100-40-6

PRINT ISBN: 978-1-945100-54-3

PRINT: 979-8-402385269

Copyeditor: Erica Ellis – inkdeepediting.com

SUMMARY

Claire's once-in-a-lifetime dream vacation to Italy turns into a hellish nightmare when she's mistakenly caught up in a dangerous smuggling situation. Thankfully, her reliable lifelong best friend is there to help her out of the mess she's fallen into.

Justin has had a crush on his best friend since grade school. The only problem is that it is obvious to everyone but her. But now that they're halfway around the world, dealing with some very dangerous men, he figures it is past time he showed Claire just how he feels. Before it is too late.

PROLOGUE

Claire Stein's life was over at thirteen. Or at least that's what she thought as she watched her mother drive away with Claire's older sister Robin for the last time.

What the heck was she going to do now? She wiped the tears that blurred her vision of the empty street outside her childhood home in Castle Rock, Colorado. The home where her parents had raised her and Robin since birth. The only home she and Robin had ever known. What was her sister going to do in California without her?

Robin was the only ally Claire had ever had in life.

"Well, it looks like it's just you and me Claire-bear," her father said, putting a hand on her shoulder.

She jerked away and turned on him. "This is all your fault," she screamed. Even as the words left her, she knew they weren't true. After all, it wasn't her father's fault her mother had fallen for some yoga instructor online and had decided to divorce the bear of a man who stood looking down at Claire now with nothing but concern and love in his eyes. But Claire's teenage hormones had been at full alert since she'd had her first period three months before, so she stomped her foot and glared up at the gentle giant. "If you'd cared more about making your wife happy than working all the time, maybe Mom wouldn't have left you. Then the stupid judge wouldn't have sent Robin away to live with that whore."

"Be careful." Her father's soothing voice cracked a little. "She's still your mother."

"No, she isn't," Claire screamed. "I hate her. I hate you. I hate Robin for leaving. I hate...." A sound close to that of a wild bobcat caught in a trap escaped her lungs. She threw up her hands, turned, and bolted, running as fast as she could. She heard her father calling after her, but she didn't stop or even slow down.

She was thankful she'd spent the last two years in track and had several blue ribbons hanging on her walls to prove that she could outrun anyone in town.

Since her logical mind wasn't working properly, she ran to the one place anyone who knew her would look. It was stupid of her, and years later she would be thankful for that stupidity. But for now, she rushed up the dirt road behind her home until she reached the summit.

There were many hills in this part of Colorado, but only one the town was named after. Claire had always imagined that when the first settlers came to the area, the rock had been a symbol of a new hope and a new home. Now, the thing was ugly and covered with cell and radio towers.

If she wanted to, she could climb to the top of the jutted-out rock. She and Robin had done it a dozen or more times. But for now, she settled in the dry dirt that surrounded the red stone and pulled her knees up to her chest and cried.

"Wow, what's all that for?" a boy's voice said from directly behind her.

Jumping a little, she glanced behind her and saw Justin Cardone hanging on the rock cliff a few feet above her head. Justin was a year above her in school.

As far as looks went, he'd won the lottery. He was tall, at least six-two, and had dark olive skin thanks to his Italian heritage. That jet black hair of his was something she'd dreamed of having herself. Or at least running her fingers through.

Claire had been stuck with wiry blonde locks that curled in all the wrong places. Her sister Robin had won that lottery in her family, with her longer honey colored hair that would do anything her sister wanted it to.

She hadn't expected Justin to be up on the hill, as he usually spent his summers helping his parents out at their restaurant in town, A Taste of Italy. The glossy pictures of Italy on the wall of the restaurant were the reason Italy was top of her list to visit after she graduated.

She had been so focused on her anger when she'd rushed up there that she hadn't even seen him hanging there. She knew that he and his father often came up here to go climbing, like a lot of other locals in town.

She'd known the Cardones her entire life. Nicky, Justin's sister, was in a couple of her classes. The family lived less than a mile from her home. Actually, when they'd been younger, she, Robin, Nicky, and Justin had been very close friends. Justin was probably the closest thing to a best friend that Claire had ever had. She hoped that wasn't going to change now that Robin was gone.

"Go away." She buried her face in her hands again, but she was so concerned about what he thought of her, her tears instantly dried up.

She heard a few pebbles being dislodged as he either continued climbing up the rock face or moved back down towards her. Either way, she wanted him to just leave her alone so she could wallow in her own pity.

She wanted to peek and see what he'd done, but before she could, she heard his voice right next to her.

"Is it about your sister moving?" Justin asked.

She wiped her eyes and then glared at him and said, "Leave me alone."

Justin smiled and wrapped an arm around her. "Claire, how long have we been neighbors?" She sighed and rolled her eyes. "No, don't answer that." He held up his other hand. "I'll enlighten you. Our entire freaking lives." He chuckled. "We both know that our parents used to bathe us together." He bumped his knee against hers.

"Go away," she said again, only this time there was no conviction in her tone.

"Did Robin and your mom leave already?" Justin asked.

She sighed and closed her eyes. "I hate them all."

"Why on earth would you want that sort of negative energy to follow them to California? Not to mention the hurt and guilt your dad must be feeling. Not only for losing his wife to some... leotard-wearing California pansy..."

Claire smiled and even chuckled.

"But for losing a daughter too," Justin finished.

Just hearing those words made her insides sink in despair. Justin was right. This wasn't her father's fault. He was a victim just like she and Robin were. It wasn't Robin's fault the judge had split them up. If she could, she would have followed her older sister anywhere.

Sure, they sometimes fought, but they were going to conquer the world together. Robin was going to be a famous movie star, and Claire was going to make her look good while doing it.

"You're really good at talking and stuff," she said, nudging Justin's knee back. "You should be a shrink or something."

Justin laughed at that. "Yeah, right, just call me Doctor Justin. I'll solve all your problems."

CHAPTER ONE

Italy... Ten years later

Claire stepped off the train and took a deep breath. She coughed at the stench of smoke from someone who had walked by her with a lit cigarette. Still, it didn't dampen the view of the sun rising in Venice.

Okay, so the view was that of a train depot, but still, it was better than the view she'd had at the airport when she'd arrived shortly after five in the morning.

She picked up her luggage and followed the small crowd of people to the main terminal. When a set of narrow steep stairs blocked her path, she lifted her luggage and maneuvered down them, trying not to topple over.

Thankfully, she'd decided to travel light. One medium sized roller bag and a backpack so stuffed that her shoulders ached from the weight.

But her luggage wouldn't be an issue once she checked into her hotel. She would be spending a whole week in

Venice. Then she'd hop on a train for Milan, where she would soak up as much fashion as she could for an entire week. Then there was a quick two-night stop in Florence before she headed on to Rome for the rest of her month-long trip. She held in a squeal as she walked.

In the main depot, she stopped at a vendor and purchased a sparkling water and a large croissant stuffed with chocolate for breakfast.

This was her time. She was going to do all the things she'd dreamed of for years. And it had all been made possible by Robin.

Now that her sister was a full-blown A-lister in Hollywood, she'd purposely worn several of Claire's designs to a few choice events. That had allowed her to finally afford her dream vacation, an entire month in Italy.

It took her no time at all to walk to her hotel, since she'd chosen one that was close to the train station. She didn't want to carry her luggage all through the canals or worse, try loading it on a shuttle boat. Actually, her hotel overlooked the Ponte degli Scalzi stone bridge and was tucked behind a seventeenth century church that she simply had to stop and take several pictures of as she passed both of them.

She walked down a narrow walkway and through a green courtyard and checked in with the clerk in the lobby area. Her room overlooked a small canal. Very small, but still, it was water.

After freshening up and changing, she opened the door and stepped out into the fresh mid-day air. She was going to stop at the very first gelato place she found and absolutely pig out.

That first day in Venice, she followed the narrow pathways over so many small walking bridges that she lost count. When she was hungry, she stopped and ate. When she was tired, she found someplace to sit, usually in a square near a fountain or along the water, and watched the tourists rush by her.

Her hotel bed wasn't as comfortable as they had boasted, but it was a place to rest her head. Besides, so far, she hadn't spent a lot of time in the small room.

Her second day she was a little more organized. She had marked several places on her cell phone map that she wanted to visit. She spent the entire day strolling through the museums, historic gothic churches, and some other famous sites all over Venice. She ate, rested, and enjoyed every minute of it.

She got an early start on the third day and planned on spending some of her saved up money at some local shops, including something special just for herself.

For the first hour, she just walked around the narrow alleys and pathways, taking hundreds of pictures with her phone. She stopped at every single gelato place, or so it seemed, getting sample sizes so she could find her favorite flavor and shop.

It took her over an hour to wind her way through Venice and make her way to St. Mark's Square. She sat along the water and watched all the boats coming and going as she sipped on a coffee. It was her second time in the square during this trip. There was so much to see here, she could easily spend the rest of her day having lunch and walking through each small store, no matter what they sold, just to see everything.

After strolling through the shops for a few hours, she purchased a rose-colored lace scarf for Robin and a blue one for herself.

She was so tempted to purchase some of the colorful glass sold in many of the stores but had planned to spend her fourth day touring the island of Murano. She wanted to watch the glass being blown herself and then purchase direct.

She found a small café that overlooked the port to sit and have lunch. She couldn't help herself from going a little crazy and ordering a large plate of pasta with mussels, garlic, and parsley. She ate the entire bowl while sipping on a glass of wine. The way she figured it, she was walking everywhere and had easily hit her daily steps before lunch, so she could afford the carbs.

The meal reminded her of Justin, and she felt a wave of guilt wash over her. The last time she'd seen him, they'd fought. Having a sexy Italian god as a best friend wasn't good for her sex life. Especially, when he treated her like a little sister instead of a friend.

She'd shown up at his family's restaurant already a little tipsy. Why not? After all, she'd walked there from her studio apartment in town. It was only three blocks away. She'd been celebrating the fact that, thanks to her sister, Carolyn Collins had requested one of her designs for the Emmys. The freaking Emmys.

Sure, Robin had worn a couple of her dresses to a few award ceremonies, but this was Carolyn Collins. Daytime goddess. One of Claire's all-time favorite characters in her favorite drama series, *My Life on the Wire*.

Showing up at Justin's family restaurant drunk and ordering more drinks and breadsticks at the bar hadn't really been a good idea. But then the handsome tourist had walked over and bought her more drinks. She'd tried to flirt with him but had seemed to be failing miserably.

She hadn't even realized Justin was behind the bar at first, that was how far gone she was. But when her drinks started being exchanged for water, she realized quickly what he was doing.

She'd complained to Justin, but that hadn't gone over well. Shortly after, the hot guy she'd been flirting with ... disappeared. That had pissed her off even more.

She'd finished the evening off by storming out of the restaurant and marching home in a huff. What she hadn't realized at first was that Justin had followed her to make sure she got home safe. When she'd spotted him under the streetlight, she'd marched up to him and shoved a finger into his chest and had blamed him for her lack of a sex life.

Her face heated now as she thought about it. She'd tried very hard to keep her feelings for her best friend to herself. Over the years, she and Justin had had many arguments, as friends did. Most of them were because she was a complete klutz and had gotten into some sort of trouble, and he had stepped in and solved it without complaint.

However, that night, he'd complained plenty on the walk back to her loft. She'd yelled at him that she was thankful she was leaving the next week for Italy and that maybe she'd find some rich Italian millionaire to marry and become a famous designer and never return.

He'd paled, and Claire had instantly wanted to take back her words. He'd just finished walking her home in silence. Once she was safely inside, he'd left without another word.

She hadn't spoken to him since and somehow her heart hurt even more now.

She shook off the sour mood. She was in Venice! This was no time to think about Justin or her past. Here, she could be or do anything she wanted.

She'd been so lost in her thoughts; she'd wandered down a back alley. There was a shop there that sold masks, the kind Venice had made famous. The Carnival of Venice had ended a few months ago, but at least she could bring home one of the stylish masks to hang on her wall.

She walked in and smiled at the clerk, greeting him with the Italian she'd been practicing for the past three years. He was a man in his mid-thirties, and he looked annoyed that she'd entered the shop.

The man responded with a quick, "What does the lady want." Or it could have been, "What do you want." His accent was too thick to really tell.

"I'm just looking," she said in chopped Italian.

"Hurry, I'm closed," the man replied.

"Oh." She bit her lip and instantly saw the mask she wanted. The brightly colored jester mask was to her the ultimate symbol of Venice Carnival. It had bright pink and purple flares on its head, complete with gold bells hanging from each flare. The face was multi-colored and had pink lips with gold outlines. She instantly fell in love.

Without thinking, she snapped a few pictures of the shop and the mask. She'd taken so many pictures that day that it was almost second nature. She wanted to remember every detail of her trip. Even if it meant constantly uploading the images to the cloud.

"I'll take that one," she said in English, pointing to the mask just behind the man's head.

The man's eyes narrowed at her and asked in Italian, "You are the American?"

"Yes," she said, sighing with relief. She was having a difficult time

"You are... the American?" he asked in English this time. His English was as choppy as her Italian.

"Yes, I'm American," she said again, then she switched to Italian. "How much?"

The man seemed to relax slightly as he ran his eyes over her. "You are not as expected."

She glanced down at her green khaki pants, her white shirt and black blazer, and the black sandals she'd put on before heading out. No matter what anyone said, she knew how to put an outfit together. Had the man never seen an American before? She was sure she'd seen several other tourists wearing vaguely the same attire throughout the day.

"How much?" she asked again in Italian.

The man reached up and removed the mask. "One hundred euros."

She bit her lip. She'd been hoping to pay less, but seeing the mask up close, she really, really wanted it.

Nodding, she took her purse out and counted out the cash she'd exchanged at the bank at the airport.

"I'll wrap it for you," he said, taking the cash and then disappearing into the back. She glanced around at the rest of the masks as she waited. Some of the masks were downright scary looking. Some had long white noses, black eye holes, and eerie grins that gave her the creeps. There was one that had three faces, and another designed as a daemon. She glanced at her clock to hide the shiver that raced through her.

"Here you are," the man said when he returned. "I assume you know what to do now," he said in English.

She took the large bag that held her boxed-up mask and smiled. "Thank you."

She practically glided all the way back to her hotel. Her third day in Venice had been a huge success.

Tomorrow, she was going to jump on a shuttle to Murano and spend the entire day exploring the smaller islands. She'd spend some money, get a few gifts for her father and sister, and enjoy herself completely.

Now all she had to do was drop off her loot at her room before finding a place to eat dinner near her hotel. She was looking down at her phone to try and find someplace to eat when she turned the corner to her hotel and bumped into someone.

"Sorry," she said, glancing up. She didn't register what was wrong with seeing him there until she moved past him, and he called to her. Then it dawned on her. She was in Venice. She spun around and glared at him.

"What in the hell are you doing in Venice?"

***

Madison Hayes strolled towards the tacky mask shop on her bright yellow three-inch heeled boots. She wore the skin-tight black leather pants that she'd purchased on her last trip to Paris. Her entire outfit cost more than the building she was standing in.

Thanks to her daddy, Madison had never wanted for anything. Her father's family owned one of the largest makers of weapons in the world. It had started back with Madison's ancestors, who had started making weapons for the Spartans. Then, after many generations, they'd started making guns and moved from Greece to the States. Shortly after the family started Hayes Industries, they became a powerhouse in weaponry, and one of the wealthiest families in the world.

As she opened the door, a dull short-haired blonde woman bumped into her. The woman's outfit was straight out of any American store. Standard clothing for a standard-looking woman.

"Sorry," the woman said in English before disappearing.

Madison gave her no more thought as she stepped inside.

Marco was supposed to be here. Where was he? She stomped her foot and glanced around.

"Hello-o?" she called out, impatient.

A younger dark-haired man appeared. Upon seeing her, he frowned.

"May I help you?" he asked in Italian.

"Yes," she replied in perfect Italian. "Where is Marco?"

The man's eyes narrowed. "My brother had to run an errand."

She shifted her special edition Versace handbag. "He was holding something for me."

"You are... the American woman?" he asked.

"Yes," she said in English, growing impatient. She had a dinner date with Lorenzo, the man she'd decided would get all her attention this trip. She'd met him at the train station and had decided, upon seeing all his muscles, that he would be her Italian lover for this trip. She was only in Venice for three nights and didn't think anything about inviting the man back to her family's villa.

After all, she always took a lover when she was overseas.

"There must be some mistake," the man said. "I..." He motioned to the door. "I gave what you need away to the other woman."

"What woman?" She frowned, remembering the boring blonde.

"She was just here." He pointed to the door.

Madison's heart jumped. If she didn't bring the list to Carmine, he was going to kill her. Rushing to the door, she glanced out and looked around for the woman. The alley was empty.

Taking a deep breath, she knew what she had to do.

Knew that if she didn't, she'd be held accountable. Besides, she really enjoyed this part.

She closed the shop door, flipped the lock, and reached into her handbag. She pulled out her "Shusher," what she called the gold-plated Beretta 9mm that her daddy had given her for her last birthday.

"I'm sorry... I thought..." the man started to say. Then he gasped and gripped his chest. Watching his face, she smiled as the red blood gushed out from between his fingers.

"Shhh," she said with a smile as the guy dropped to the floor.

She stood over the man and waited impatiently until the gurgling noise stopped. Then she pulled out her phone and called Rubio.

"Rubio, I need a maid." She glanced towards the door, wondering how hard it was going to be to find one tacky American tourist in Venice.

CHAPTER TWO

J ustin knew it was borderline stalker of him to show up at Claire's hotel in Venice. Hell, he'd meant to tell her the last time he'd seen her that he would be in Italy at the same time she would be. But then she'd flirted with that jock and... hell. He'd forgotten.

She'd been telling everyone she knew about her trip for months. If he'd mentioned his own trip, it would've looked like he had planned it on purpose.

He'd only meant to check in on her. Or so he'd told himself. But the truth was, he'd wanted to see her. To apologize for acting like an ass the last time he'd seen her.

He'd done everything he could to control his feelings for her his entire life. But seeing her hanging all over that muscled creep had set him off.

"I—" He started to answer Claire, but then she stopped him by lifting her hand.

"Tell me you are not here," she said, closing her eyes for a moment.

Did she think his company was that bad? Hadn't they

been friends all their lives? Did she hate him so much now that she was upset that he was there during her vacation?

His gut twisted as he waited. When she opened her eyes again, she sighed.

"Why are you in Venice?" she asked finally.

"I… meant to tell you that we were going to be here, but it slipped my mind. My cousin is getting married," he answered quickly. "Honest, the last time I saw you, I was going to—"

"Your cousin? Isabella?" she asked as she titled her head.

"Yes." He smiled. "My parents were set to come with me, Nicky as well, but she's off somewhere on a story." He shoved his hands into his jean pockets.

In the last year, Nicky had taken a job as an investigative journalist for a large online news provider. Their parents were so proud of her traveling the globe, writing about it, and seeming to live her best life.

"Your mother told me about the wedding." She sighed and seemed to relax. "I guess it slipped my mind that the wedding is here." She glanced around as if his entire extended family was hiding in the alley somewhere.

"It's the day after tomorrow." He added. "At Chiesa di San Giorgio Maggiore," he added. "When I mentioned to Isabella that you were in Venice for a few days, she suggested I ask you if you'd like to attend."

"Isabella's wedding?" She ran her eyes over him. He nodded again. "The day after tomorrow at Chiesa di San Giorgio Maggiore? In Venice. The same time I'm here on my dream vacation," she repeated as if trying to understand everything he'd just said. Her eyes narrowed, and he could tell that she was thinking, "It's a small world, huh?"

He nodded and sighed. "I wanted to tell you, but..." He looked down at his shoes. "It slipped my mind."

"Okay," she said suddenly. She straightened her shoulders and turned away and started walking towards a bright blue doorway.

"Okay?" he called after her.

She glanced over her shoulder. "Yes, I'll go with you." She stopped just outside the door. "I'm going to drop this stuff off and then go out for dinner. Got any plans?"

For a moment, his brain just wouldn't work. No, he didn't have any plans. Beyond attending his cousin's wedding and reception.

He'd arrived yesterday and had pretty much been busy with catching up on his sleep. He'd been so jet-lagged, that he'd taken a nap after lunch.

When he'd woken, he'd headed here and had spent almost half an hour debating whether to find which room she was in and surprise her or face the wrath of her finding out he'd been in Venice after they returned from the trip. That thought had sent a wave of shivers through his body. He did not want to face Claire's wrath again. Not after the other night.

He had just convinced himself to text her that he was in town and leave it in her hands when she'd bumped into him.

"No plans," he admitted.

"I'm too happy to argue about anything. Come on." She started walking and motioned for him to follow her.

They walked through the brightly lit door into a small courtyard. "Nice," he said as she made her way towards a set of stairs.

"Yes." She smiled over her shoulder. "It's one of the

reasons I picked this place. That and it was close to the train station. Where are you staying?"

"The Gritti Palace." He almost bumped into her when she stopped at the top of the stairs.

"A palace?" She looked confused and impressed at the same time.

"It's called that. It used to be a palace of sorts, now it's a hotel." He shrugged. "Just like this one." Okay, so the place he was staying at was nothing like this one, but he didn't really want to go into it. Since the room had been reserved for him, his parents, and his sister, they'd gotten a full suite. He had more room than he knew what to do with.

He was not just partly Italian. His family came from and was still in Italy. Most of his cousins lived a few hours from Rome and had connections with hotel and restaurant owners. So, when he came to Italy, which he had done a lot in his life, his family had always taken care of accommodations. His room was part of the whole wedding package his cousin had arranged.

Normally, it would have been his entire family attending the wedding, but his mother had twisted her ankle last week and was walking with a crutch. There was no way his father was going to deal with her side of the family without her, and Nicky was on assignment somewhere and couldn't get the time off, so he was there by himself.

"Where is this palace?" she asked, unlocking a brightly colored door.

"By the Piazza San Marco," he answered while she put down the shopping bags she'd been carrying. She ran a brush through her hair, looked at herself in the mirror, and added some fresh lip gloss.

He watched her, mesmerized by her movements. He'd

wondered how she got her lips to be so... juicy looking. How many times had he lost track of what she was saying, just because he was watching those lips? Dreaming about sucking on them. Tasting them.

"I just spent the day over there," she said. She must have continued to talk as she walked towards him, but he'd been so focused on those lips, he hadn't heard a word.

She stopped in front of him and looked at him, her eyebrows arched up in annoyance.

"Sorry?" he said.

"Ready?" she asked with a smile.

"Yeah, sure." He stepped aside so she could lead. He followed her back down the stairs, through the courtyard, and back down the narrow alleyway. She stopped when they entered the main pathway.

"Where to?" she asked, glancing over her shoulder.

He knew a few good places near his hotel, but in this part of Venice, he wasn't too sure. Glancing around, he shrugged and pulled out his phone. "Let's take a look."

She leaned against the wall as he scanned his phone. He knew what he was looking for. Someplace on the main thoroughfare but not too busy. In the end, he ended up texting Isabella and asking for a place.

She suggested a local dive, a place that they were guaranteed to have the best food in Venice, or a high-dollar place that would impress Claire.

Every fiber of his food-snob ego told him to pick the first. But, in the end, he went with the restaurant along the water.

"Find a place?" Claire asked as he straightened from his position of slouching along the wall while he read his text.

"Isabella found us a place," he corrected with a smile.

"Come on." He took her hand and rushed across the bridge, crossing the canal.

"Where are we going?" Claire asked when he turned the corner and started heading along the water.

"We're going to grab a ride." He motioned to a gondola.

"On that?" she asked, her tone going up slightly.

He laughed. "You aren't still afraid, are you? I pushed you in the lake once when we were twelve." He chuckled as her eyes narrowed at him.

"What's to say you won't do it again?" she asked as they stopped in front of the gondola.

"First off, I'm not twelve. Second, this is Venice." He motioned around with a smile. "If I pushed a woman off a gondola, I would be known as the least romantic man on earth."

She chuckled and nodded. "Okay, I'll trust you this once."

They settled in the seat, and he talked with the gondolier in Italian while Claire listened closely.

As they started to move, she glanced over at him. She gripped her purse tightly, as if it was protecting her from falling into the water.

"I'd forgotten you speak fluent Italian," she said.

"It's been the second language in my house my entire life," he reminded her. "How are you getting along here? Did that language app my mother suggested help out?" he asked her, remembering she'd asked for his help with a few translations while she'd been learning Italian.

"Some." She shrugged. "I'm obviously not as good as you, but I'm making do so far."

As the gondola started moving down the narrow channels, they settled back and watched the scenery pass by them. Claire took several pictures before she spoke.

"I'm sorry," she said, avoiding his eyes.

"For?" He knew that she was talking about last week. But he also knew her well enough to understand that she wouldn't be able to focus on anything else until she'd had it all out.

"I was drunk." She shifted slightly, looking at him. "I was celebrating and well..." She sighed and then titled her head. "You were cock-blocking."

He almost choked on air and finally managed, "Excuse me?"

Her chin rose as she crossed her arms over her chest. "You heard me."

He wasn't quite sure how to respond to that. "I'm..." He thought about it quickly.

The truth was, he'd known she liked the attention the jock had been giving her that night. But moments before Claire had walked into the restaurant, he'd heard the asshat boasting to his friends about being able to bang the next hot piece of ass that he bumped into.

He'd thought the man an ass to begin with, and then he'd started flirting with Claire, his Claire, and... she'd flirted back. He didn't know which pissed him off the most.

So, he'd done what any testosterone-driven, sex-deprived male would have done. He'd acted like a complete ass.

"I'm the one who should be apologizing," he finally said. "I allowed my distaste for jocks to cloud my better judgment."

Claire's eyes narrowed as she looked at him. "You always have hated jocks," she said with a slight smile.

He smiled. "Long-standing issue from junior high."

She laughed. "Do Kurt and Bobby still give you shit when they're around?"

He shrugged. "Not since I started outlifting them at the gym our senior year. But that doesn't stop me from keeping my distance."

Her smile slipped. "I always hated them when they ganged up on you and gave you a black eye."

"Broke my nose." He reached up and touched the slight bump on the ridge.

"I think it makes you look ... sexier," she admitted. It was the first he was hearing this, and his eyebrows shot up at the confession.

"Oh?" He leaned a little closer. "What about the scar they gave me in middle school during a soccer game? Right here." He pointed to his elbow.

Her smile grew as she looked at the little white line. Then she said in a low sexy voice that had his libido jumping into full swing, "Very sexy." She practically purred it.

Suddenly, all the years of friendship blurred as his feelings for her, the ones he'd tried to squash for years, surfaced and took over.

Claire Stein. The girl—the woman—he'd always loved was finally looking at him as something other than a reliable best friend. And he'd be damned if he was going to pass up the opportunity to show her just what they could be together.

CHAPTER THREE

What was she doing? Flirting with Justin. She could see the flames of desire in his dark eyes. The same look he'd given Katy McDougal in middle school when he'd lusted after her.

Then she blinked and her heart skipped a full two beats. No, the look he was giving her was nothing like what he'd given Katy.

Swallowing the lump of desire, she blinked and glanced over his shoulder.

"Where are we going?" she asked, breaking the trance.

Justin glanced over as their gondola made a turn down an even narrower canal. There was barely enough room for one narrow gondola now as they continued onward. She was sure that at any moment, the wood of the gondola would scrape against the stones of the walls surrounding them.

Justin pulled out his phone and looked at the map.

"It's just ahead. It opens up into the Grand Canal soon." He relaxed back.

"How many times have you been to Venice?" she asked him, curious.

She knew that he'd taken an almost yearly trip to Italy with his family. After all, his grandparents were first-generation Americans. His grandfather had moved his family to the States shortly after his father was born. His mother's side was basically the same story. The rest of both of their families still lived in different parts of Italy.

"Venice?" Justin asked and then thought about it. "Two or three times," he answered with a shrug. "Maybe more that I can't remember as a kid."

"What's your favorite place to visit in Italy?" she asked, trying to hide the nerves that had surfaced suddenly. It was funny, she'd never really been nervous around Justin before. She'd have to think about why she was now when she was alone.

"My second cousin's place just outside of Rome. They took over managing the family's olive grove a few years back. It's one of the most beautiful spots I know." He voice was laced with wistfulness.

Just then the gondola pulled out into the Grand Canal, and she quite literally lost her breath. "Even more beautiful than this?" She nodded to the view of the sun setting over the water and the red-tiled sandstone buildings that surrounded them.

"Close," he said, his eyes never leaving her face.

Again, she felt her insides jump at his look. Why was he doing this to her suddenly? Maybe she was a little more jet-lagged than she'd thought? Food and sleep. That's what she needed.

She kept telling herself that as they made their way towards the bank and climbed out of the gondola directly outside the restaurant.

She pulled out her wallet to pay, but Justin beat her to it.

"My treat," he said as he took her hand and walked towards the entrance of Ristorante Venezia. They glanced at the menu before being seated at a small table on the water's edge.

She listened as he talked fluently with the waitress, and she could have sworn that he was flirting with the brunette, but then the woman handed them each a menu and disappeared. She'd caught a few words: wine, time, and something about a couple.

"There, this is nice." He motioned to the view of the Ponte Di Rialto footbridge. She'd crossed the bridge earlier that day and had enjoyed the little shops along the way.

"Yes," she agreed. She could just sit there all night and watch the tourists coming and going.

"What are you in the mood for?" he asked, looking down at his menu.

She glanced at it and then pushed it aside. "You decide. I trust your judgment." She returned her gaze to the bridge and the water. It was fun watching everyone enjoying gondola rides. There was a young couple, fully clothed in eighteenth century costumes, getting their pictures taken along the water, which was gaining a lot of attention.

The woman's dark red dress with cream colored lace was straight out of a movie set. Her dark hair was braided and tucked under a matching hat. The man wore a matching outfit of short pants, a long jacket with a white frilly shirt, and a hat so big that she wondered how much it weighed.

"Isn't it amazing?" she asked Justin, who glanced up from reading the menu.

"Hm?" he asked. When she motioned to the couple, he

glanced over. "Oh." He smiled. "Yeah, I'm so thankful pantaloons haven't made it back in style."

She laughed. "There's something romantic about the women's dresses, but the thought of wearing a corset..." She visibly shivered. "I have a difficult time just putting on a bra most days."

His dark eyebrows shot up and then he did something she'd never seen him do before. He glanced down at her chest as desire flooded his eyes once again. Instantly, her cheeks heated.

"God, I'm wearing one now," she said quickly. She could feel herself blush even further when he chuckled and glanced back down at his menu.

Thankfully, the server was back. She set two glasses down and held out a bottle of wine for Justin, who nodded after seeing the label.

When the waitress poured them each a glass, Justin gave her their order in Italian.

"What are we having?" she asked when they were alone again.

"Italian," he answered with a smile as he took a sip of the wine.

She rolled her eyes. "You're such a food snob." She took a sip of her wine. God, it was good. How did he know which wine to order? Whenever she went somewhere, she always just ordered the house wine and was satisfied. Not that it was ever as good as this wine. She turned the bottle towards her and frowned.

"Cardone... as in... Your family makes wine?" she asked. "Why am I just finding this out?"

"I don't know. We have it at our restaurant. You've had it plenty of times. Why you've never looked at the label is a mystery," he added sarcastically.

She playfully nudged him under the table. He was always teasing her about her lack of attention to detail. She tried to slow down and pay attention, really. But having ADHD meant that she often jumped from one thing to the next before anything could sink in.

"Okay, so, your family owns an olive grove and a winery. Not to mention the restaurant back home." She leaned on the table and looked at him. "What else?"

"My family owns just the restaurant in Castle Rock. My dad's family owns the olive grove, the winery business, and several large holding companies all over Italy. My mother's family owns..." He shifted slightly. "A lot more."

She leaned back. "You come from money," she said in an accusing tone.

"No. My parents do. Nicky and I spent most of our youth busting tables," he replied.

"And spent at least a month each year traveling all over Italy." She crossed her arms over her chest. "Do you know how long I've dreamed of coming here?"

He smiled. "I think you started complaining about not being able to fit in my suitcase when you were eight."

She smiled, remembering the time he'd been packing for a family trip during the holidays, and she'd dreamed of stowing away in his luggage.

"And I finally made it here. Only to have you show up at the same time."

"I showed up a day ago," he pointed out.

She rolled her eyes. "The point is, you're here at the same time."

"My whole family would be if my mother hadn't been trying to hang a picture over her sofa and twisted her ankle jumping off said sofa," he pointed out as the waitress set a basket of bread and two small plates of flavored oil in front of them.

"Right," she said again, instantly feeling bad about his mother, Camilla, whom she called Cammy for some reason. She'd worried when she'd seen her hobbling around in a large black boot. "How is Cammy doing?"

Justin smiled at her use of his mother's nickname.

"She's fine. Sad to miss the wedding, but also kind of happy, I think. She loves Isabella but isn't too pleased with Matteo and his family." Justin rolled his eyes and then dropped into a thick Italian accent like his mother used. "The Esponsito family and the Cardones don't mix. There's too much bad blood in our history. Besides, everyone knows that the Esponsito family comes from a long line of Italian mafia. Some say they still dally in espionage. Mark my words, me amore, the marriage won't last a year."

Claire couldn't help but smile at Justin's impersonation of his mother. It was spot on.

"What do you think? Is Matteo good for Isabella?" she asked. The last time she'd seen his cousin had been a few years ago when they'd still been in high school. Isabella was a few years younger than they were and was always fun to hang out with. They'd had fun teaching one another curse words.

"I only just met the man last night briefly. But from what I've seen so far…" he shrugged. "He dotes on Isabella."

"Lots of men dote during the first few months of a relationship. But after the initial glow fades…" She took another sip of her wine.

She thought about the last two relationships she'd had and how both men had changed weeks or months after the relationship had started.

"Josh?" he asked, breaking her out of her memories.

"Him and Corey, not to mention Timmy."

"Timmy..." He thought about it then laughed. "What was that? Second grade?"

"Hey." She pointed at him. "He promised to marry me when we were ten. Then a week later, he promised Sara Lindberg the same thing."

Justin laughed. The rich warm sound had her smiling. "What about you?"

"Me?" he asked. The laughter still filled his eyes, making them sparkle.

"Sure. I'm sure you've promised loads of your exes the world. What about... Megan? Why exactly did the two of you break things off?" she asked, leaning on the counter.

His laughter slipped just a little. "She cheated on me with Dan."

"What?" She straightened up. "I thought..." She shook her head. Megan had spread a rumor through town that the breakup had been mutual. That they had just grown apart. At the time, Justin had seemed over it, so she'd never asked him.

"Yeah." He sighed. "So did everyone in town. Except Dan," he added dryly. He smiled. "I suspect he knew the real reason."

Claire smiled. "Sorry. I suppose I should have gotten the whole story from you instead of relying on rumors."

He shrugged. "I was over it almost immediately. We'd only been dating a few months."

"Months." She dragged the word out. "The longest relationship I've had is three weeks." She held up three fingers. "Three."

"Yeah, we all know about your commitment issues," he teased her, making her smile again.

"Not all of us are lucky enough to be on the top ten list," she said, relaxing back.

Justin groaned. In the local dive bar back home, there was a list hanging on the bulletin board. No one knew who'd started it, but one day almost two years ago, a "Top ten hottest available males and females in town" list showed up.

Everyone in town was eager to see their name on the list. At first, she'd been a little upset that she hadn't appeared on the list. Then she'd been upset when her name appeared a few months later after one of the previous women had run off and gotten married.

Justin's name had remained in the top three since the list's creation.

"Someone ought to burn that list," he said with a groan.

She smiled. "They have. Several times. It keeps reappearing." She leaned forward and narrowed her eyes at him. "There were rumors going around that you created the list to put yourself on there. I mean, you did spend a whole year in the number one position."

"There's a rumor going around that your sister started the whole thing. Since the list appeared during one of her visits," he countered.

"You're not Robin's type. She would have never put you in the top position." She smiled.

"I don't know. There was a time, before she moved away, that she had the hots for me," he said with a smirk.

"She did not." Claire gasped, and instantly knew that he was poking fun at her and decided to hit back. "You're not sophisticated enough for Robin."

He chuckled. "No one is sophisticated enough for your sister. I heard she is dating a senator now."

"What?" Claire sat up straight. "Oh, Blake." She'd just

talked to her sister earlier that day. Robin was in Paris filming a movie called *It Takes Two* with super sexy movie star Tom Levi.

"Blake Rhodes," Justin said, sounding impressed. "Senator Blake Rhodes."

Claire's eyes narrowed. "Robin says he's really nice. I'm not sure it'll last. She's dated the rich and famous before," she said, making air quotes around the word *dated*. "Most of the time, it's media hype."

"This time it sounds serious," Justin pointed out.

She pulled out her phone but then stopped, knowing her sister valued her privacy above all else. If she was dating the sexy senator, Robin would tell her on her own terms.

"That was a quick change of mind," Justin joked. "You two still on good terms?"

"Yes," she sighed. "I'll message her later."

"What about Nicky? Is she seeing anyone while she jets around the world?" she asked.

"Nope. She claims she's married to the job," he answered with a shrug.

Just then, four large plates of food were set on their table: a massive pile of pasta with sausage and red sauce, another with dark sauce and fresh mussels, one with creamy sauce, and a pizza with fresh vegetables on top.

"This... is a lot of food. Trying to fatten me up?" she joked.

"Never. You're perfect the way you are." He smiled as he poured her more wine.

CHAPTER FOUR

H e hadn't expected for dinner to go so perfectly. The food was great, and the location was as romantic as his cousin had hinted at. As usual, getting along with Claire was something that came easy. Not to mention fun.

They were so much alike and yet different enough that their conversations never seemed dull. After he'd mentioned seeing a tabloid about her sister and Senator Rhodes, she'd grown quiet for a time.

Maybe it was due to their food arriving, but he wondered if she and Robin were getting along. Even though she claimed their relationship was fine, he knew they'd had issues after Robin had moved to California with their mother.

He remembered how she'd felt all those years ago when she'd stormed up the hillside and sat below him, crying. It had broken his heart, but part of him had just been thankful she hadn't been the one to move away.

Now, as they walked back to her hotel after dinner, Claire talked about her plans for her trip. He'd suggested they catch another gondola ride, but she'd suggested walking instead.

She even wrapped her arm in his, like she always did as they walked.

"What are your plans? I mean, are there any big wedding events you have to attend?" she asked as they crossed yet another small footbridge.

"The rehearsal dinner is tomorrow night."

"What about tomorrow during the day?" she asked, biting her bottom lip as she pulled out her phone and tried to take a picture. It was too dark and after trying a few times, she gave up. Then she surprised him by pulling him close and taking a selfie of the two of them.

For a full minute after, all he could see was the flash from her camera, which had blinded him. She'd taken his arm again and continued walking like the bright light hadn't fazed her.

"So?" she asked as they turned down another narrow passage.

"Hm?" He'd lost track of what she'd been talking about.

"Tomorrow during the day."

"Oh, no, nothing going on. The rehearsal and dinner start around seven," he replied as they crossed the last bridge.

"What do you say to breakfast? I can meet you at your hotel and we can go from there?" She turned down the walkway to her hotel.

"Okay," he agreed, trying to hide the eagerness from his tone. "I'm in room two-twelve."

"Eight o'clock?" she suggested, and he nodded. "The Gritti Palace?" She stopped at the blue door and pulled out her phone. She searched the map and pinned the location.

"Gotcha." She smiled up at him. "Thanks for going with me to dinner. I probably would have picked someplace that was overpriced with not very good food."

He chuckled. "It pays to know people who know people," he said in his best Italian mobster voice.

Claire rolled her eyes. "You can pull off your mother, but you are no Don Vito Corleone."

"No one can pull off Don except the one and only Marlon Brando." He crossed himself and had her laughing.

"I'm glad you're here," she said, then she turned around and quickly disappeared through the door.

Nothing could have made the evening better, he thought as he started back towards his own hotel, opting to walk the entire way. Except if he'd grown balls enough to kiss her. Hell, he hadn't had the balls for the past twenty-four years. What made him think he could even dream of it now just because they were in Venice?

Maybe because it *was* Venice, the city of love. Since the moment that he'd found out he would be in Venice when Claire was, he'd dreamed of how it could be. How he would finally be able to show Claire how he felt about her.

When he finally made it back to his hotel room, he fell face-first onto the bed and dropped off immediately.

He woke to knocking on his door. He stumbled out of bed and opened the door to his suite to Claire. She stood on the other side of the door in a brightly colored skirt, a soft low-cut white shirt, tan boots, and a straw hat.

"This is nothing like my hotel," she said, walking past him into the sitting room of his suite. "Seriously, you think my small room comes close to comparing to this?" she asked, motioning around the room. She pointed into one of the two bedrooms. "Seriously?" She walked over to the glass doors that led to a balcony overlooking the Grand Canal. "Seriously." She shook her head at him, as if she was disappointed.

He wasn't quite awake enough for a conversation, so he walked into his room, grabbed some clothes, and disappeared into the bathroom without a word.

After a long hot shower and a shave, he dressed in khakis and a button-up shirt. He stepped out of the bathroom just as a cart of food was being rolled into the room towards the balcony.

Claire tipped the woman after she arranged the meal on the table that sat on the balcony, then followed her back to the door to shut it behind her.

"I thought we were going out for breakfast?" he asked as he stepped out onto the balcony after Claire.

"That was before I realized just how awesome of a place you're staying in." She motioned to the view again. "I doubt we could find a place to eat breakfast with a better view if we tried." She sat down and poured them each a glass of orange juice.

He shrugged and poured himself a cup of coffee and added cream and sugar.

"I forgot that you're basically a Neanderthal until you've had a cup of coffee," she said cheerfully.

"I'm Italian," he replied, as if that explained everything. He took a slice of bacon and shoved it in his mouth.

"I've met plenty of Italians. I'd wager every single one of them is friendlier than you are in the morning," she teased him.

It wasn't until his second cup of coffee hit him that he looked, really looked, into her eyes. He knew instantly something was wrong.

"What?" He sat up a little, reaching for her hand. "What's wrong?"

Robin set down her mug and sighed. "I talked with Robin last night. You've heard about everything she and Blake have gone through in the past few weeks?"

He nodded, remembering someone shooting at them in Paris, then a bomb going off at Blake's place just outside of Paris, the Château de Ferrières, where Robin and her crew had been filming the movie Claire's sister was working on currently.

After that, he'd lost track of what was going on.

"She didn't really want me to tell anyone, but... you're family. I'm sure it's all over the news at this point." She shrugged. "I haven't had the heart to watch any more about it. She was kidnapped last night." She held up her hands. "She's okay. Blake and his security team shot and killed the man. His brother is in custody."

"Where?" he asked, concerned. Surely, if Robin had been hurt, Claire would have been on the first flight out.

"At Blake's place in Georgia. I wanted to go home, but she convinced me..." she shook her head and closed her eyes — "no, she threatened that she would never forgive me if I left." Claire smiled slightly. "Besides, she says Blake is taking good care of her."

"Is she okay?" He felt slightly uneasy just thinking about it.

"Yes, she's okay. I don't think she's telling me everything but..." She sighed.

"Surely something like that is all over the news this morning?" he asked. He hadn't had time to check yet.

"I don't know about this morning, I didn't look. But Robin wanted me to keep as much as I could quiet. She assured me that they were okay and not to worry." She frowned. "Nothing can remove the worry."

"Sounds like dating a US senator is dangerous," he suggested.

"This time... Robin thinks they were after her." Claire bit her bottom lip, a move he knew meant she was seriously worried. "She's had a few stalkers in the past."

"Someone's after Robin?"

She nodded and closed her eyes. "Take my mind off it. She's assured me she's safe. She's surrounded by Blake's family, and she said some pretty scary-looking security guys are there to make sure of it, but still..." She opened his eyes. "Take my mind off of hopping on the next flight to Georgia."

"Okay," he agreed. He started talking about Isabella's wedding. He told her that the rest of the family was staying at the same hotel, and she mentioned the idea of hanging out with them.

"They're meeting with the caterers this morning, then off to grab their tuxedos," he answered. He had reserved his at a different store and it wouldn't be ready until the next day. He was glad. He wanted to spend the day alone her. He'd pretty much convinced himself on the walk back to his hotel room last night that he was going to finally make a move.

What the move was, he had yet to figure out.

"Okay, so then..." She bit her lip and glanced out over the water. "I was planning on hopping on one of those tours that go to Murano and seeing how the famous Venetian glass is blown."

"Sounds good." He finished off the last piece of bacon. "I've yet to head out that way myself. We can catch one of the tour boats down there." He motioned towards the piazza. "I think that they have shuttles that leave every hour."

She practically jumped out of the chair and rushed towards the door. He followed a little more slowly. After grabbing his wallet and putting on shoes, he locked the room up and followed her downstairs.

As they passed the lobby, he heard Claire say, "Seriously?" under her breath as she shook her head. He smiled all the way to the boat.

They only had to wait fifteen minutes before they were shuffled onto the boat along with almost twenty others. The trip out to the island took roughly half an hour, during which he and Claire talked about everything except for her sister.

She told him her hopes and dreams for her future, then she asked about his.

He mentioned his parents were pushing him to take over the restaurant, since they wanted to retire and start traveling more.

He liked the idea, really. He'd been raised in the place, knew the ins and outs of it, and loved every part of running the place.

While Nicky had always had her head in writing her stories, he had consumed everything he could about the family business. He had ideas of his own as well. Maybe expanding. Opening another location closer to Denver.

"That's a great idea," she said when they docked. He helped her stand up, keeping his hand on hers to steady her since the boat was swaying and bumping against the dock.

"In theory, but we'll see if I can find a building and if we can save up enough money to move forward. Starting a new business, as I'm sure you're well aware, is costly." He helped her out of the boat, and they followed the rest of the tour group into a large red brick warehouse.

"I'd be starting from scratch. You're lucky that you have a successful business already," Claire mentioned. Then all conversation stopped as they listened to the tour guide.

He had to admit, watching the glass worker, or vetraio, was pretty interesting. The man made a delicate unicorn like it was as easy to him as breathing.

A half hour later, the group was shown into the sales room, where he and Claire spent another half an hour shopping.

Claire was looking at shot glasses when he spotted the case with the jewelry.

When he saw the glass heart pendant on a delicate eighteen-karat gold necklace, he knew instantly he had to purchase it for Claire. The interlaced bright colors mixed with gold flakes in the heart reminded him so much of her personality. Bright and cheery, with many different moods, mixed with the pure gold of her heart.

After paying for the pendant, he found Claire paying for some blue hand-decorated Murano shot glasses for her father.

"Dad is going to love these shot glasses," she said, motioning to the glasses. "They'll ship them directly to him, so I won't break them, knowing my luck," she joked as they started walking around the shops on Murano.

"That's a smart idea. I would've never thought to send things home. I usually just cart it all through the airport with me."

"I'm in Italy for just over a month," she said cheerfully. "With what I've already purchased, I'd be carting around another suitcase already. Sending everything home is the smart move."

She stopped at a wood bridge and glanced out at the water. Pulling out his phone, he snapped a picture of her.

She laughed and turned towards him. "What was that for?"

"It's the perfect backdrop."

Claire glanced over her shoulder at the brightly colored homes behind her. Then she leaned on the railing with a sigh. "It's so pretty here. As if we stepped back in time."

He moved beside her. "Venice hasn't changed much over the years," he agreed. "It's not like they can build a new mall or a Target," he joked.

She took a deep breath and closed her eyes. The sight of her relaxing had his body jumping to attention. With every fiber he had, he knew it was the best thing to do, to tell her how he felt.

She looked so perfect in the sunlight, her blonde hair glimmering like the surface of the water. Her cheeks were sun kissed, and her lips had that sexy gloss over them again, making him want to have a taste.

"I got you something," he said suddenly, holding up the bag with the box inside that held the heart.

Claire turned to him; her eyebrows arched in question. "For me?"

He nodded as she took the bag. He watched in silence as she opened the box.

"Oh!" She gasped slightly and then smiled as she pulled out the glass heart. "It's beautiful." She glanced down and smiled.

He reached into the box, removed the heart, and motioned for her to turn around. "It reminded me of you and goes with your outfit perfectly."

She lifted her hair as he clasped the gold chain around

her neck. Thoughts of brushing his lips over the pulse in her throat surfaced, so he took a step back.

Her fingers brushed the glass. "I love it." When her eyes lifted to his face, he stepped forward until he was an inch away from her.

"I've wanted to do this my whole life," he said. Then he pulled her into his arms and kissed her.

CHAPTER FIVE

W here the hell had this come from? Claire asked herself the moment Justin's lips touched hers. Then she switched to asking. Why the hell hadn't this happened sooner?

Her entire body started vibrating when Justin's lips touched hers. Then he dipped his tongue into her mouth, and she practically melted against his chest. Her arms reached around and she gripped his shirt in her hands.

Just as quickly as he'd kissed her, he stepped away from her.

She wasn't sure what to say and stood there, looking at Justin as if seeing him for the first time. She'd never believed she had a chance with someone like him. Over the years, the raging crush she'd had on him had fizzled into friendship, even though secretly she knew she'd never be happy with being just friends. She'd been jealous of any woman who had earned his attention and still held a grudge against anyone he'd dated.

Seeing Justin smiling back at her, she took a deep breath as he took her hand in his.

"Well, you didn't slug me. I'll take that as a good sign." He started to walk. "How about we grab a coffee and some gelato?"

Not trusting she wouldn't say something stupid, she nodded and followed him into the nearest gelato shop.

"Did I break you?" he asked once they were sitting on a bright red bench, eating their gelato as they watched the water.

"No." She shook her head and smiled. "A woman can be dazed after something like that," she admitted. He chuckled.

"So can a man." He nudged her knee with his own.

"Sooo." She dragged out the word. "You've been wanting to do that for a while?"

He nodded. "You?"

She nodded and took a bite of her dulce de leche gelato, her favorite flavor so far. She had tried Justin's caffè flavor and, though it was good, nothing beat the caramel taste.

"I used to dream about that happening," she admitted, avoiding his eyes.

"What changed?" he asked.

She chuckled and glanced over at him. "You started dating Lily Beck."

He was silent for a moment then smiled. "Fifth grade?"

She nodded. "You would walk through the halls holding her hand."

"If it's any consolation, I wished back then that it was your hand I was holding." He took her free hand in his.

"Where do we go from here?" she asked once they were done with their gelato.

"Well, I was thinking we could finish walking around here, hop a boat back, sit through my cousin's rehearsal and dinner, then maybe see how we feel," he answered.

She'd been asking about them. How was this going to change their relationship? What did he expect? What did she expect?

"No, I mean…"

He lifted their joined hands to his lips and brushed a kiss over her knuckles.

"I know," he said with a chuckle. "We've had twenty-three years together so far. I think we can take a little time to figure out the future."

She nodded in agreement and followed him through a couple more shops, where she purchased a few more trinkets for her family or friends.

He even purchased a little something more for his cousin. Sure, his parents had shipped the family gift long before the wedding. No doubt his aunt and uncle would have it wrapped and piled with the rest of the gifts at the reception.

But this little something was from him personally. The small keyring of a cat licking its balls was the perfect gag gift. He also got a key ring of a wooden gondola for himself. Claire liked it so much, she grabbed one herself.

Less than an hour later, they were settled on a boat heading back.

"Do I need to change for tonight's dinner?" she asked him, worried that it was a little more formal than her skirt, top, and boots.

"You're perfect. I'm going as is." He motioned to his burgundy shirt and tan pants.

"You look Italian." She nudged him. "No denying it. Me?" She glanced down. "I'm in tourist uniform."

He chuckled at that, then reached up and touched the glass heart at her throat. "You'll bring the sparkle to what I expected to be a very boring evening."

She couldn't argue with that. The boat dropped them off at the same place they'd gotten on, by the hotel—scratch that, the palace—he was staying in.

They walked slowly back to his hotel, holding hands, and passing through the crowd of tourists.

She couldn't believe how beautiful his hotel was. They stepped into the lobby area with its dark rich wood, marble floors, and beautiful art and glass work everywhere.

Justin said something briefly to the two men behind the counter, who nodded and smiled at her.

They headed up the three-story marble staircase and to his rooms. He unlocked the door and motioned for her to step in. Once again, she was enamored with his room.

It was a beautiful mix of the old and new. Stylish grey and white furniture filled the sitting area, and glass and crystal hung overhead. Long white curtains allowed for the corner room to be shadowed in darkness if wanted. For now, each of the five French doors showed an amazing view.

She'd loved sitting out on his balcony, watching the boats come and go as they'd eaten breakfast. If possible, she would have breakfast right there every morning for the rest of her trip.

She realized she hadn't asked him how long he would be in Italy. She turned to him. "How long are you staying in Venice?"

"I'm here for three more nights. Why?"

She smiled. "I'm here for three more nights too."

He smiled and took her hand. He walked towards the doors and stepped out onto the balcony. "Then it looks like we'll have plenty of time to enjoy the sites together."

"Sounds wonderful." She sighed and looked out over the chaos beyond. "Oh!" She stood up. "I should have gotten Isabella a present."

Justin chuckled. "Your being there is present enough. Or so she claimed when she insisted that I invite you."

She relaxed back and leaned against the railing as she ran her eyes over him.

"She seemed pretty sure I'd come then?" she asked.

He nodded and leaned sideways, his eyes on her. "She remembered you instantly. Claims you're the reason she can now curse like an American sailor. Her words, not mine."

Claire laughed. "Guilty. She's the reason I understood what the man was screaming at the train station when he missed his train."

"My parents taught me both English and Italian curses... Not by choice." Justin smiled.

"Your dad does curse a lot when he's cooking. Your mother curses whenever you do something that pisses her off."

"Which is all the time," they said together. They both laughed.

"We're Italian. Hot blooded, fiery, and—"

"Hardheaded?" she interjected. He smiled.

"Passionate." He pulled her close and kissed her again.

Yes, there was plenty of passion in his kiss. Enough that, once again, she found herself leaning on him heavily just to remain upright.

"Wow, do you have a license for that kiss?" she asked as he trailed his lips down her neck.

His chuckle vibrated his chest. It took her a moment to realize it was her cell phone buzzing in her pocket.

"My sister," she said after a moment. "She said she was going to call..." He nodded as she answered.

While her sister filled her in on more of the details of what had happened at the Château de Ferrières and Blake's place in Georgia, Justin walked over and pulled out his computer. Then she talked about Blake and Claire instantly knew that her sister had lost her heart.

She'd never heard Robin talk like she did about Blake, which assured her that it wasn't just a relationship hyped up by the media. The thought of her sister actually finding her one had her watching Justin closely. She wanted to tell her sister about the day they'd spent, about her feelings, but since he was sitting in the room with her, she got off the phone without letting her sister in on the major change in her life.

"How's Robin?" Justin asked as they headed to the rehearsal.

"She's okay. She's resting. Everything that happened to her is all over the news."

"Yeah, I've seen a few pictures of her and Blake flash on TV screens. I'm happy she's okay."

They walked towards the boat taxi that would take them across to the Chiesa di San Giorgio Maggiore.

She was in awe the moment she saw the large white building. There was a clock tower in the back and a large dome that she couldn't wait to see the underside of.

A small group of people stood outside and when they got closer, she recognized Isabella immediately. The woman, upon seeing them approaching, rushed over and wrapped her arms around Claire.

"It's so wonderful that you were able to come," Isabella said cheerfully. "When Justin told me you were in Venice..." She made a happy sound. "Fate."

She was dragged through the large black doors of the church. Just seeing the inside of the beautiful building, she knew that it was going to be an epic wedding.

Not only was Isabella going to make a very beautiful

bride, but she was also so kind and friendly with everyone. Isabella was no bridezilla. She laughed and joked with everyone as she hung onto the very handsome Matteo, who didn't speak a word of English and looked at Isabella as if she were a goddess.

At one point during the rehearsal, she caught Justin looking at her much the same way. How many years had she dreamed of being with him? Of what it would be like being part of his family.

Hadn't she tried to sneak to Italy on one of his family trips several times?

Being best friends with the man she'd secretly desired her entire life, no matter how hard she tried to deny it, had been the worst. But now, knowing that he felt something for her... it was as if she could finally start dreaming.

She dreamed the entire time he stood up in front of the church as a groomsman, while the priest droned on in Italian.

When the rehearsal was over, they all rode in a large taxi back to the hotel.

"The rehearsal dinner is on the hotel's bar lounge patio," Justin said, taking her hand and helping her out of the boat. God, she loved it when he touched her.

There were more than a dozen tables on the patio, which hung out over the water. It was different than the patio area for the restaurant attached to the hotel. Both had a beautiful view of the Basilica di Santa Maria Della Salute, with the sun setting behind it.

The sky was a brilliant orange and pink, and even Justin pulled out his phone to take a few pictures of the scenery.

They took a seat with his cousin and Matteo and another couple that Claire found out was Matteo's sister Melissa and brother-in-law Gabriel Belli, who, thankfully, spoke enough broken English that Claire didn't feel too left out.

"Tomorrow's reception is up on the roof restaurant," Isabella said to her. "I hope the sunset is as beautiful as tonight's."

"So far, every sunset I've seen here has been better than the last," she said.

"So, you two?" Isabella said, leaning on the table and adding an eyebrow wiggle.

Justin looked over at Claire with his eyebrows up, as if he was trying to think.

"Have been friends all our lives," Claire said happily. "And nothing could ever possibly change that." She took Justin's hand under the table and gave it a light squeeze.

Isabella's eyes narrowed as her smile grew. "I've always been rooting for something more between you."

"You have?" Justin asked with a slight frown, then he looked at her again and she felt her heart pound uncontrollably at the way he looked at her.

"Yes, there's obviously a spark. I mean, everyone else can see it," Isabella joked.

Claire smiled over at Justin. "Whatever is here, one thing is sure. We're going to have a fun time exploring Venice."

Justin smiled back at her. "Agreed."

CHAPTER SIX

S itting through the dinner was like waiting until the end of a sermon. Not that he didn't love spending time with his cousin, but he wanted to kiss Claire again. Wanted to hold her, to tell her how he felt. How he'd felt for a very long time. But instead, he sat across from his cousin and tried desperately not to focus on the tingle he got each time Claire's leg brushed up against his or she held his hand.

He wanted more than anything to be alone with her again.

"You got quiet," Claire said after their empty plates were removed.

"Just counting the seconds until I can kiss you again," he whispered into her ear.

Seeing her face flush and her eyes dip to his lips had him smiling.

"We can have dessert elsewhere?" she suggested. "Maybe some gelato on the way as you take me back to my hotel?"

"That could work." He nodded to Isabella. "I'll make our excuses."

Fifteen minutes later, they were on a boat taxi, heading back towards her hotel. Thankfully, they were the only ones on the small boat and the moment they left the dock, she leaned against him. Just wrapping his arms around her made him feel more centered.

"Can I tell you how much I'm enjoying you being here with me?" she said with a slight sigh.

He smiled. "You can."

"I don't know what I'm going to do when you leave. Not that I hadn't planned on this whole trip being awesome without you, but..." She sighed.

"This changes things." He looked down at their joined hands.

"Yeah." She sighed again. "It does."

"The question is... is it a good change?" He held his breath until she answered.

She leaned away to look up at him. Her eyes danced with humor and a spark of something else he recognized as lust. "I'm willing to find out if you are."

As an answer, he cupped her chin and leaned down to kiss her.

They docked near her hotel and slowly made their way down the narrow cobblestone pathway until they ran into a gelato shop.

He grabbed one of his favorites, limone flavor, and wasn't surprised when Claire opted for the same. They sat on a bench along the canal and enjoyed the cold treats while they talked about his cousin.

"Oh god." Claire gasped. "We're going to a wedding tomorrow, and I only brought one other dress. It is in no way appropriate for a wedding."

"Then go shopping in the morning," he suggested. She

looked at him as if he'd grown a second head. "What?" he asked with a shrug. "It is Venice. They have dress shops."

"Yes, I know they have shops, but..." She bit her lip. "I'm working on a budget here and, as you said, it is Venice. I have three more weeks in Europe, and I didn't want to blow my entire budget in the first few days."

He thought for a moment then smiled. "So move in with me and save your hotel fee." She laughed. He waited until she was done laughing to add, "What's funny about that? It's a smart idea."

"I am not moving in with you." She shook her head.

"Afraid I snore?" he joked. He could already see her questioning the decision.

She laughed again. "I know you snore."

He frowned as he remembered the summer trip they'd taken with a group of friends. "I had a cold."

"Right," she said between chuckles. Then she stopped laughing and tilted her head. "You do have a two-bedroom suite."

"Exactly," he said with a smile. "Did you think..." He dropped off as he took her hand.

Her eyes moved to his. "No." She shook her head. "I mean..." She bit her bottom lip, and he felt his insides shift like they always did when she made that slight unconscious move.

"Claire, we've known each other our entire lives. This shouldn't be a thing. Come, use my parents' suite with me. Stay in your own room or don't." He smiled. "It's up to you."

"All right," she said after a while. "But I'm going to drag you shopping with me in the morning."

He groaned slightly. He knew what shopping with Claire was like. "You're a clothing snob."

She laughed. "You're a food snob, so there's that. It will

take me as long to pick out a dress as it takes you to order appetizers."

He chuckled. "I'll hold you to that." He stood up. "Let's go check you out and get you moved over."

They walked back to her hotel, and he sat there while she packed up all of her things. Thankfully, she was as tidy as she was, and it didn't take too long. That was another thing they had in common. He knew it was for different reasons—she was a clothing designer, and he was just a neat freak.

It was hard to explain, but that was just one more reason he'd fallen for her long ago.

After they loaded her luggage on a water taxi, Claire searched on her phone for clothing stores near his hotel.

"I'm only doing this for the dress," she said when they stepped into the room.

"The dress?" he asked as he set her luggage down.

"This dress." She showed him the screen of her phone. He took her phone as she wheeled her luggage into the spare room.

The rose-colored dress had spaghetti straps, multi layered frills, a hip-hugging waist, and a long skirt with a slit to showcase those sexy legs of Claire's. It was so like her; it was as if it was made for her.

"See, you already found the dress." He handed the phone back when she walked back into the sitting room.

"Yes." She beamed at him. "They're even holding it for me." She glanced down at the phone and then hugged it to her chest. "I wouldn't have been able to afford it." Her eyes moved up to him. "If it weren't for you."

"Don't thank me. Thank my parents," he said, feeling a little guilty. He'd invited her to stay with him for selfish reasons. He wanted her close, needed her close. For as little or as much time as he was allowed.

"Justin." She laid her hand on his arm. "Just take the gratitude."

He nodded, then held in his breath when she reached up and kissed him.

"Claire." Her name slipped from his lips as his hands moved down to her hips and pulled her closer.

When she pulled back, her eyes fixed to his, he knew that no matter what happened between him and Claire, there was no going back. For them, they had already crossed the line beyond friendship.

They'd probably crossed it years ago, without even noticing. Long before they'd ever kissed. For him it was a no-brainer. He loved her. Always had. Always would.

Did she feel the same way? If so, how long had she felt this way?

"I can see what you're thinking," Claire said with a smile. "The answer is yes; I really do want to head in there." She motioned to the bedroom as her eyes moved over his face. "See what it's like to be with you."

"But?" He saw her hesitation now and knew that he too had questions.

"I need to know that nothing will change between us," she said.

He chuckled. "Sex changes things between people, no matter what."

She sighed and rolled her shoulders. "Yeah, but it doesn't have to change..." She motioned between his heart and hers. "We've been friends. No matter what, we remain so."

"Agreed," he said firmly.

Then she was kissing him again and pushing him towards his bedroom. He wanted to tell her to slow down, but his body was doing the thinking at this point. He wanted her too much.

Plus, she was rubbing herself against him. Just the feeling of her soft breasts against his chest had the air frozen in his lungs.

It took no time at all before their clothes were lying about the room as skin finally pressed against skin. Just gliding his hands over the soft skin over her ribs had him harder than he'd been in years.

"Claire," he groaned as she stood before him in a matching silk bra and panties in a soft blue.

"Justin." She smiled up at him as she reached down and slipped his pants from his hips. She smiled when he sprang free, then she brushed her hand against him, and he had to bite his lips to stay focused.

"You're killing me," he groaned as he reached for her. Then he frowned when she took a step back and chuckled.

"You're not supposed to be frowning." She reached behind herself and unclasped her bra.

Everything in his life focused. Everything he'd ever wanted, ever done, disappeared. His life focused on this one moment in time. On Claire.

He'd seen her in bikini tops plenty of times. Hell, once, in high school, he'd seen her in a bra. But never had he seen her like this. She was everything he'd ever dreamed. Perfect.

From her short blonde hair to her pale blue painted toenails.

"If you keep looking at me like that..." She smiled as she walked closer. "This may be over far too early."

"Never," he said, reaching for her. "I'm going to do what I can to make this last. I want to savor every moment. Every touch and kiss."

He leaned down and kissed her. He wanted to touch her but held back. When she took his hand and carried it up to her breast, he felt his heartbeat triple.

Claire groaned as he ran his hands over her. He'd never experienced anything like the way Claire responded to his touch. She was right, if he didn't slow down, this was going to be over far too soon.

He had to take control. Then she started sliding her fingers over him, and he knew he had to do something. He lifted her up in his arms and carried her to the bed, where he softly set her down.

When she reached for him, he smiled, but instead of settling over her, he shifted to settle between her legs, using his hands to nudge them farther apart.

"Justin." His name was a warning.

"Easy," he said before kissing her through the sexy blue panties. "I'm going to enjoy this."

Her hands went into his hair as he enjoyed himself. She smelled like spring, felt like the silk that covered her, and tasted... He pulled the silk aside and dipped his tongue across her.

She jerked under him, and her fingers tightened in his hair. "Justin," she cried out when he did it again, this time slower.

"Come for me, Claire," he said against her skin.

He didn't have to ask again. When he dipped a finger into her and ran his tongue over her, she cried out his name and gave him what he wanted.

CHAPTER SEVEN

W hat the hell was that? Her eyes were closed tight, and she was trying to focus on breathing to settle her heart.

She thought she'd been schooled. Thought she'd had experience, as far as sex went. She was dead wrong.

Yes, sex with Justin had changed things. How was she supposed to know ahead of time that it would be so... powerful? And all he'd done so far was use his tongue and fingers on her.

She opened her eyes and focused on his face as he moved between her legs.

"Claire," he said softly before kissing her.

She pulled him down further as he settled into her. It was as if she'd been missing a piece of herself and, finally, everything in her entire life was finally right.

She wrapped her legs around him and held on, giving him everything she had. Everything she'd ever felt for him. She'd wanted to get her hands on him for her entire life and now she enjoyed running her fingers over his toned body.

"Let go," he said next to her ear as he trailed his mouth down her neck.

Her entire body convulsed under his touch. How was it that she bent to his will so easily? As stars exploded behind her eyes, she felt his release and tried not to scream his name as he softly moaned hers.

Her heart ached by the time she recovered this time. How was she going to tell him what she felt? Could she? Should she?

"Claire?" he said as his weight pinned her to the mattress.

"Hm?" she asked, her fingers lazily making circles on his back.

"I lied," he said, not moving.

"Hm?" she asked, tensing slightly.

He shifted until he looked down at her. His darker eyes searching hers.

"This changes everything," he finished with a smile.

She smiled back. "Yes," she agreed. "It does."

He kissed her slowly, and she felt him grow hard against her. "I want you again," he said between kisses.

"Me too." She pushed her fingers through his hair and lost herself once more into him.

She woke to the sound of her phone ringing.

Justin groaned as she rolled out of his arms and looked at her screen.

"Who is it?" he groaned.

"No one, it's my alarm. I promised the shop I'd be there first thing when they open up." She tried to roll out of the bed, only to have him pull her back down and cover her with his body. He kissed her until she relaxed back and once more enjoyed being with him.

"I'm blaming you for being late," she said once they stood in the massive shower together.

He chuckled as he ran his soapy hands over her back. "Since we're going to be late..." He placed a kiss on her shoulder, and she melted against him.

"Don't," she said, but she didn't put too much energy into it. Then her second alarm went off on her phone. He sighed and stepped back.

"Your second alarm," he said, and she turned in his arms and nodded. It was nice being with someone who knew her so well. Tom, her last boyfriend, had been annoyed at her persistence and punctuality.

Justin kissed her, rinsed them both off, and turned off the water.

"Later," he said as he handed her a towel. His eyes heated as he watched her step out of the shower naked. "Later," he said again. This time his voice was lower, almost a growl.

She felt her knees go weak as she wrapped the towel around her.

She dressed quickly as Justin ordered room service. It was only after he'd poured his second cup of coffee that she realized he hadn't been a total ogre that morning.

Smiling, she said to him, "So, not just coffee can improve your mood in the morning."

He chuckled. "Italians are driven by two great forces." He wiggled his eyebrows.

"You keep making those excuses." She looked down at her phone as it rang. "My sister again." She answered as Justin stood up and disappeared inside.

"So, how's Venice?" Robin asked.

"Wonderful," she said, watching him disappear inside. "Justin is here."

Robin was quiet for a moment. "On purpose?"

Claire laughed. "He's here for his cousin's wedding, and we bumped into one another. Well, Isabella asked him to come invite me to the wedding today."

"Oh! How exciting," Robin exclaimed. "An Italian wedding." Her sister sighed.

"How are you feeling?" she asked Robin.

"Much better."

"And Blake?" Claire asked, leaning on the table.

"He's... perfect," Robin said with a deep sigh.

Claire's eyes moved to the doors where Justin had disappeared.

"I slept with Justin," she blurted out.

"What?" her sister said. Then she added, "It's about damn time."

Claire smiled. Robin had been telling her for years to just yank that Band-Aid off. But Claire being Claire, she had doubted Justin's attraction to her. She'd believed for years they would always be stuck in the friend zone.

"Whatever happens now," she said, watching Justin walk across the room, heading for the doors again, "I'm all in," she added as he stepped back outside. "Justin's here," she said, switching the phone to speaker. "Robin." She motioned to the phone.

"How's Georgia? I hope better than they're saying on the news," Justin asked easily as he sat back down and placed his phone on the table. That must have been what he went back inside for.

It was so nice dating a man that her family already knew and loved. They chatted for a few minutes before Robin had to go. Then they headed out to the small boutique just off the square to purchase her dress. She didn't even have to try it on, really, to know that it was perfect for her. The soft color accented the slight tan she'd gotten the day before and magically made her boobs appear larger.

Since she had saved enough money from the hotel room, she purchased a pair of nude-colored sandals to go with the dress. She had a white handbag that would go perfectly, along with some silver hoop earrings, a bracelet, and a necklace.

The wedding started in a few hours, which gave them plenty of time to pick up Justin's tux before heading back to the hotel to change. Along the way, they stopped at a café and sat along the canal to have some more coffee and some chocolate croissants since they would be skipping lunch.

When they returned to the hotel room, she took her dress into the other room while Justin disappeared into his own room. Taking her time, she recurled her hair and touched up her makeup before slipping on the dress.

When she stepped out of the room, her breath caught at the sight of Justin in a tux. She'd seen him dressed in a suit before, but never a tux. The man oozed sex appeal.

"Wow," she said, motioning for him to spin with her fingers.

He chuckled and turned slowly. Then he made the same move for her. She smiled as she turned, letting the skirt of the dress twirl.

"Wow," he agreed as he walked towards her. He placed a soft kiss on her cheek and smiled. "Don't want to mess up the lips," he said as he looked at her perfectly glossed lips. Then he held out his arm for her to take. "Shall we?"

Smiling, she took his arm, and they walked out and caught the first water taxi.

"Is there anything I should know about your family?" she asked as they headed across the water.

He thought for a moment. "My great-nonna, Sophia, is a liar," he said with a smile.

"Your great-grandmother is alive?" she gasped.

"Yes, on my mother's side. One of my nonnas on my father's side will be here too. The two women have been best friends since..." He shrugged. "Forever," he finished with a smile.

"Is that how your parents met?" she asked.

"My parents have known each other since they were in diapers." He looked over at her. "Like us."

She chuckled nervously as the taxi docked, and Justin helped her out of the boat.

"Here goes," she said under her breath as they walked across the square towards the growing crowd near the entrance of the church.

"Since I'm in the wedding party, I'm going to have to leave you in my family's hands during the ceremony." He approached a group of people. "Anything they say about me is all lies," he joked as he stopped near the group.

For the next half hour, she was introduced to what seemed like every member of his extended family. So many faces and names were tossed around, but she held onto a few. His great-nonna, his nonna, his aunt Louisa and uncle Ralphio, Isabella's parents, and Justin's other cousin Dante Cardone, who looked so much like Justin, it was uncanny. The man and his wife, Airlea, along with their twin daughters, Camilla and Cora, invited her to sit with them during the ceremony.

Airlea had dark caramel skin with long dark hair that flowed over her shoulders. She wore a light peach dress that matched her husband's tie and her daughter's dresses perfectly.

She enjoyed talking with Airlea while the ten-year-old

girls played with their many cousins in the square and everyone waited for the call to shuffle into the church.

"If you have time during your trip," Airlea said in perfect English, "you must stop off and visit us at the olive grove. We're just a couple hours outside of Rome."

"I'll be in Rome my last week," she said. "If I have the time, I'd love to visit. I've always wanted to visit your home. Justin has told me so much about your place and business."

Airlea smiled. "We've heard a lot about you and your famous sister as well."

Just then, the family was called to take their places, since guests were starting to arrive. The music started playing, and she was showed to where she would sit with Airlea and her family.

For the next hour, she took in everything, from the bridesmaids' cream-colored dresses to Isabella's beautiful off-the-shoulder silk and lace wedding dress with its long, beautiful train. She'd given a lot of thought to her own wedding, since clothes were of the utmost importance to her, but she'd never imagined anything like this before.

Justin looked extremely handsome up there with the rest of the men and looked comfortable, as if he'd stood in at many weddings before. She was finding it difficult to peel her eyes away from him. The more she looked at Justin, the more she realized just how long she'd been in love with him.

After the happy couple walked down the aisle together to the many cheers of the guests, she went to join Justin out front where the rest of the wedding party stood around talking to guests. Justin was talking to a raven-haired woman.

The woman was not only beautiful but flawless in a very tight, short red dress that showcased an impressive pair of double D's. Her legs were extremely long and fit and accented by a pair of red spiky heels that made her almost the tallest person in the crowd. The closer she got to them, the more she noticed about her.

Her lips were triple the size of her own, reminding her that she should have reapplied her own lip gloss before stepping outside. She was wearing a pair of dark sunglasses, but Claire was almost positive that her makeup would be flawless underneath.

When she looked closer, though, Claire noticed that the woman had obviously had a lot of plastic surgery. That stood out as much as the inappropriate tight red attire.

Stopping beside Justin, she looped her hand in his arm. He stopped talking to smile at her.

"There you are," he said with a smile as his hand rested on hers. "Claire, this is a friend of the Esponsito family from New York." He motioned to the woman. "This is Madison Hayes."

Madison couldn't believe her luck. "How absolutely wonderful to meet you," Madison said in a breathy tone as she tried to contain her joy while she assessed everything she could about the woman.

"Likewise," the dull blonde woman said with a slight nod.

Here she was, thinking the dull wedding might finally be getting slightly more entertaining after spotting the handsome Italian, and then he'd introduce her to the very woman that she had men hunting for all over Venice.

Her lips curled upward at her luck. "Claire?" Madison said, shaking the woman's hands. She noticed that although the woman's fingernails were clean and painted a soft pink, they were not done professionally. Tacky.

Actually, the dress Claire wore wasn't bad, but still, it had nothing on her Oscar de la Renta dress.

"Are you enjoying Venice?" Madison asked, taking Claire's arm and strolling towards the taxis.

Claire glanced back towards the hunk Madison had just been trying to convince to come to her chateau. The man was all but forgotten at this point. Here was her one chance to redeem herself with Carmine. She wasn't going to let it pass her by.

"Yes," Claire replied, her voice echoing her uncertainty.

"Oh, I was looking for someone more... American to ride with to the after party." She waved Claire's concerned look aside. "Coming, lover boy?" she threw over her shoulder with a wink.

Like a good man on a short leash, Justin followed them towards the waiting boats.

Now, all she had to do was figure out where Claire was staying and have her men break in during the party and get back what belonged to her. Easy peasy.

CHAPTER EIGHT

Justin didn't like the attention the fem-fetal was giving to Claire. Not that he was the jealous type. But he'd been positive Madison was flirting with him before Claire showed up, so his gut told him something was off.

Did Madison know who Claire's sister was? Maybe the attention was to somehow get to Robin?

The three of them road in a taxi back to the hotel, where other guests had already arrived. The entire time, Madison asked Claire questions. Oh, they were the polite conversational type, but still, Claire answered everything from where they were staying to her agenda when she was in Italy.

Claire, being Claire, spoke with excitement and listened while Madison highlighted a few choice places to visit at each location.

Claire even took notes on her phone so as not to miss a single attraction.

"I can't believe it, you're Robin Stein's sister," Madison said with a smile as she took Claire's arm and started walking towards a table near the dance floor. "Is it true she's dating Blake Rhodes? Oh! I bet you can fill me in on the kidnapping." He followed along and listened to Claire dodge all questions about her sister. When he spotted Matteo, he sidetracked.

"What do you know about Madison Hayes?" he asked Matteo, who appeared to be heading towards the bathroom.

"Maddy?" Matteo smiled. "She's rich, spoiled, and always bored," he said with a shrug as he continued heading towards the hallway where the bathrooms were.

"Bored?" he asked, following along.

"Yeah, nothing ever interests her," Matteo answered.

"Then why is she so into Claire?" Justin asked as they stepped into the bathroom.

Matteo stopped and looked at him. "Into?" Justin nodded, and Matteo's dark eyebrows shot up. "Maybe she's..." He frowned. "Nope, scratch that. You're more her type." He sighed. "Okay, not sure," Matteo said, stepping up to a urinal. "How into are we talking?"

"Very," he said, feeling the uneasiness spreading. Either she was a good actress, or Madison really hadn't known Claire and Robin were sisters.

Justin knew that Robin and Blake were having issues in Paris. The story had broken, complete with tons of rumors.

"Hm." Matteo walked over and washed his hands. Justin followed and washed his own. "I can check around if you want. Her parents were supposed to be here as well. They're friends with my uncle, but last minute, they cancelled. No one has seen her parents together for years."

"No." He sighed as they stepped back outside. "I'm probably being..." He ran his eyes over the crowd and spotted the two women. Claire was chatting away like she'd just met a new best friend, while Madison soaked up every word. "No, thanks." He made his way across the patio.

Claire was very easy to talk to and usually made friends wherever she went. But not normally with people like Madison Hayes. He knew her type. Women like her didn't find women like Claire so interesting that they hung on each word.

He took the chair next to Claire just as the music started.

Claire reached under the table and took his hand in hers and he relaxed. Then he was called up to sit with the wedding party and decided to pull Claire up with him.

"Thank you," she said when they sat at the longer table near the front of the crowd. "Don't get me wrong, it was nice talking to another American, but…"—she leaned closer — "you're the American I want to spend my time with."

He smiled and leaned over to brush his lips against her. "I was super jealous Madison was getting all of your attention."

"Oh, trust me, I was done with the conversation five minutes after were introduced."

He chuckled. "Not into the shallow type?"

She laughed. "No. My sister has the patience to deal with Madison's type. I, on the other hand…" She shook her head. "No tolerance."

"Good." He took her hand in his. "That means I'll have you all to myself again."

Over the next couple hours, they talked, ate, danced, and drank. They headed back to their room on wobbly legs, holding onto one another for support.

It wasn't the first time they'd gotten drunk together. It was, however, the first time he felt excited that he was the one taking her to bed.

They stumbled into their room, and she plastered her body up against his and kissed him until he felt his pants almost burst. It wasn't until they started stumbling towards his bedroom and tripped over a sofa cushion that they both looked around and realized something was wrong.

"What..." Claire gasped. "Someone broke into your room."

He groaned and leaned against the table to call down to the front desk. It was a quarter past one in the morning, and now he highly doubted the night would end the way they had hoped it would—both of them wrapped around one another in bed.

Instead, they met with the police, shifted through their items to see what was missing, and then spent almost an hour helping clean up the mess. By the time they fell into bed, the sun was almost coming up.

"Tell me your plans for tomorrow—I mean, today— aren't that strenuous," he mumbled.

"Breakfast in bed around noon," she said with a sigh. "Followed by a very long nap, then maybe dressing up and finding someplace nice to have dinner."

"Sounds like a plan," he said as he drifted off.

When they woke, they showered, sat out on the balcony, and ate their late breakfast as they watched boats coming and going.

"I'm glad I had all my money on me," Claire said as she sipped her coffee.

"Me too. It's a good thing they didn't get into the safe. My laptop and your iPad were in there. Still, they must have messed everything up when they couldn't get their hands on anything of value."

"I read an article once that said most hotel break-ins are from other guests or staff members," Claire said.

"Well, I think they realized they wouldn't get anything from us," he said with a yawn. "How about a walk after this?" Even though he was still tired, he wanted to stretch his legs.

"Sounds good." She leaned back in her chair, and he watched a frown form on her lips. "You leave tomorrow, right?"

He nodded. "You?"

"I'm heading out to Milan on the mid-morning train."

"You won't be back home for three more weeks?" he asked, already somehow missing her.

She nodded, then sighed. "Do you think things will change when we get home?"

He thought about it. "I hope so. I don't want things to go back to how they were before." He reached over and took her hand. "I like how they are now."

She smiled. "Me too."

"Good, then it's settled." He kissed her knuckles. "How about that walk?"

They strolled along the water's edge and stopped off for some more gelato and coffee before heading back to nap. When they woke, they dressed and found another place along the square to have dinner.

Part of him didn't want the evening to end, since they would be going their separate ways in the morning. While they ate, she talked about the rest of her trip and gave him more details about how she planned on opening her own clothing design business when she returned home.

He mentioned that the building across from the restaurant was up for lease.

"Since it's in town, it's perfect for a shop of sorts," he suggested. "You do plan on having a shop? Right?"

"I... hadn't really thought about it," she said with a slight frown. "I mean, yeah, I guess I'll have to have someplace to sell my designs locally."

"What about getting in with the right crowd in Hollywood? I know you did a few designs for Robin."

"I suppose I had hoped..." she started to say, and suddenly fear of Claire leaving Castle Rock flooded his mind. Had she hoped to move to Hollywood to be near her sister? To start designing clothes for the rich and famous? He'd listened to her talking about starting her own business for years, and as he played all those conversations over in his mind, at no point had she said the business was going to be based in Colorado.

"You don't plan on staying, do you?" he asked, his heart sinking in his chest.

"Staying?" she asked, her blonde brows arched upward.

"In Castle Rock?" he asked, dreading the answer. His gut told him the answer already. Why would someone as talented as her not want to be in California or New York? Hell, Milan for that matter.

"Why would I leave?" she asked, still frowning. "It's home."

His ears were ringing from all the blood pounding out of fear, and it took him a moment to realize what she'd said. "You're not leaving town?"

"No." She shook her head. "Did you..." She reached across the table and took his hand. "Did you think I was going to?"

"For a heartbeat." He chuckled. "Okay, I feared it for several really long heartbeats."

She smiled. "I don't plan on leaving. Mainly because I know how expensive living anywhere else is. But also, Dad is there, and Castle Rock is my home." She looked down at their joined hands. "And... you're there."

He relaxed completely, relieved, and then lifted her hand to his lips and kissed her fingers as he felt his heart soar.

CHAPTER NINE

Spending the rest of her time in Venice with Justin was pure heaven. She wasn't looking forward to leaving the next day. He would return home, while she would continue on with her dream vacation.

Next stop for her was Milan. The hotel she'd booked was no doubt going to pale in comparison to the rooms she shared with Justin. Still, she looked forward to spending as much time as she could sucking in all the details from the glorious designers and shops.

Still, she wished for a few more days with Justin. For the entire night, they lay in bed, talking about their future while wrapped in each other's arms. When the sun started to lighten their room, they made love again slowly before falling asleep in each other's arms.

She woke when her phone buzzed with her alarm.

"It's only your first alarm," Justin said, tightening his arms around her to keep her in place.

"I only set one," she told him. "I hadn't planned..." She smiled and buried her face into his warm chest. "On staying awake all night." She finished with a slight yawn.

He chuckled. "You can sleep on the train." He kissed her as he rolled over to cover her body with his again. Being with Justin would never get old. Never.

They ordered room service after they showered together. Sitting out on the balcony overlooking the water was one of her favorite memories of the entire trip.

She had even noticed a change in Justin's morning rituals. He didn't appear to be as grumpy in the morning as he normally had been.

"What?" he asked her over a cup of coffee. "What's so funny?"

She'd been smiling as she ran her eyes over him. "You are."

"Hm?" he asked, setting his cup down.

"You're smiling and that's only your first cup." She motioned with her own cup.

He reached across and took her hand. "I have reason to smile."

She thought about going on alone with the rest of her trip as she looked down at their joined hands.

"Are you sure you can't just cancel your flight and head to Milan with me?" She had meant it as a joke but could instantly tell that he was thinking about it.

"There is nothing that I'd love more, but..." He glanced out over the water. "You have been planning this trip for years. I don't want this"—he held up their hands— "to get in the way of your dreams."

She wanted to tell him that it wouldn't. That he could never, since he was part of those dreams, but instead, she nodded. She knew he had commitments back home. That his parents would be waiting for him to start taking over their business.

Not to mention, he'd probably been all over Italy and

found the travels there... not as exciting as she did. He'd appeared to have a great time with her, but she'd been so starry eyed that she hadn't really been paying attention to if he'd really been enjoying himself like she had.

"We can head to the train station together," he suggested. "My flight doesn't leave until later."

She smiled. "I'd like that."

"Why don't we finish eating, then pack up? We can hit a gelato shop along the way." He wiggled his eyebrows. "Since I know how much you've been enjoying the treats while you're here."

She laughed. "You know me too well."

A little over an hour later, they strolled along the water's edge. Every day since she'd arrived in Venice, the sun had shined. It had been perfect weather. However, today, the clouds darkened the sky, making everything dull and gray. She took it as a sign that it was time to move on. She'd checked the weather app for Milan and, thankfully, it was set to be sunny during her entire visit.

They both had their backpacks on their backs, and he pulled her luggage behind him. All of his travel items fit in his own backpack while she needed the small carry-on to cart most of her clothes and the items that she'd purchased that hadn't been shipped yet. She kept her necessities in the backpack along with a change of clothing. She'd even tucked her purse inside it so she could easily handle only the two items once she was on the train by herself. She'd read that little tip on a travel guide.

"Do you always travel this light?" She asked him when they stepped off the taxi and stopped to get some gelato at the small place a few doors down from the train station. They only had their backs turned for a second as they ordered. But in that time, a man snuck up behind them, grabbed her rolling suitcase from Justin's hands, and darted through the crowd with her signature bright pink luggage in his arms like a football.

She stood there in shock as Justin took off after the man. IN less than a heartbeat, she screamed and followed suit.

She ran until her lungs felt as if they were going to burst, her sides hurt, and her vision grayed. Her own heavy backpack bounced up and down on her shoulders as she rushed after Justin. She lost track of her location due to the thick fog coming off the water. Each alley looked like the last one, and she was so turned around that she wasn't sure she could find her way back to the station. Stopping when she could no longer see ten feet in front of her, she leaned her back against a stone wall, breathing heavily. Her phone rang, and she jumped at the loud sound.

"Where are you?" Justin asked. He sounded just as winded as she was.

Glancing around, she noticed a restaurant and told him the name.

"Stay there. I'm coming to you."

By the time he found her, her breathing was back under control. He walked straight up to her and wrapped his arms around her.

"I'm sorry," he said into her hair. "I lost him."

"That's okay," she said with a sigh. "You're safe. That's all that matters." Then she realized her new dress was inside the bag and cringed. "Thankfully, all my important stuff is in my backpack," she said, holding onto him.

He stilled and then leaned back. "That's twice," he said with a frown. Then he glanced up at the restaurant and motioned. "Let's get something to drink."

She followed him inside. They sat at the table, and he ordered water and a bottle of wine.

"I'm going with you," he said out of the blue after taking a sip of water.

Her eyebrows arched up. "You are?"

His eyes met hers as he nodded slowly. "I've been coming to Italy my entire life. Do you know how many times I've been robbed? How many times my hotel rooms have been broken into?"

"No. How many?" she asked, fearing the worse.

"None," he said with a sigh. "Either you're prone to drawing the thieves, or..." He shook his head. "Whatever the reason, it doesn't make sense."

She felt her gut twist. "Do you think it has something to do with my sister?"

"What?" He sat up a little, his eyes scanning the crowds outside the restaurant.

"Nothing," she said quickly. "It's just... something Robin said the last time we talked." He waited and then motioned for her to continue. "The two brothers that they caught. That had tried to kidnap her. She hinted that something didn't sit right. She'd had stalkers before. But... nothing like this. It comes with the territory. Being a celebrity. That's why she pays for security," she added. "Still, I hate that she's gone through what she has in the past few weeks."

"Your sister is a strong woman," he said with a smile.

"Yes." She smiled. "So strong that every time I mention shortening my trip to go check up on her, she threatens me."

Justin smiled. "So, then it's settled?" he asked. "If it's okay, I'd like to tag along."

She thought about it for a moment. "I suppose I could use the company," she teased.

"Just think, with me along, you can save enough money to buy a new wardrobe in Milan."

She laughed. "You sure do know the way to a woman's heart."

He smiled back. "I know you. You've probably been beating yourself up about losing that dress."

Her smile fell away. "Damn it," she said under her breath.

"So?" he asked again.

"If you are expecting me to say you can't go with me, you're going to be disappointed." She smiled. "I've been trying to figure out how to convince you to come along since the moment I saw you outside my hotel."

Where the hell was it? She tossed the tacky clothing aside as she rummaged through the girl's belongings. Could the girl be any plainer?

She'd already promised Carmine that she'd make the drop on time, which meant she had less than two weeks to get the list to its intended buyer. Herself. Knowing millions was on the line didn't scare her. After all, she made more than Carmine's buyer every time she sneezed wearing a skimpy outfit.

It wasn't the money that had drawn her to the game. It was the thrill and danger.

These people didn't care that she came from money. Hell, they didn't even blink at her family's wealth.

But they didn't tolerate incompetence. It had been Marco's fault he'd left his idiot brother at the shop.

Kicking the pink bag aside, she turned to Rubio. "You idiot. It's not here."

"The woman, she had a backpack," he said in broken English.

"Then I suppose you'll have to get it from her," she said calmly. The man made no move to go. "Now!" she screamed.

Then she remembered Claire rattling on about her entire planned trip. The idiot was so trusting. If Madison had prodded, she was sure the blonde ditz would have given her every detail.

As it was, she had only been trying to distract her long enough for Rubio and his men to break into Claire's hotel room and get the list. Now, however, she wished she'd paid more attention as the woman had droned on and on about her boring trip.

She turned to go but stopped. "She's heading to Milan today," she told Rubio, remembering at least that detail. Rubio nodded and started to go. "I'll be following you. I'll stay at my usual hotel. Contact me once you have the item." She dismissed him.

After he left, she turned back to the view and frowned. It was pathetic to think that, at one point, she'd taken Rubio as a lover. What had she been thinking? He was totally inept.

____

CHAPTER TEN

Sitting on the train to Milan, while Claire slept in the seat next to him, Justin used his time to rearrange his flights to match Claire's. Then he sent a text to his parents, telling him of his plans. He left out the bit about their room being broken into and Claire's luggage being stolen.

He knew they would be thrilled that he and Claire were an official item. How many years had they been hoping and hinting that they would make a great couple?

It was probably one of the reasons he hadn't made a move before. Who was he trying to fool? He glanced over at Claire as she slept, her head resting on his coat tucked between her and the glass window of the train. He hadn't made a move before because he'd been concerned that it would damage what they had.

It was too important to him. She was too important. Whatever happened, he didn't want to lose her.

"Are we there?" she asked when the train started to slow.

He glanced at the map app on his phone quickly.

"We're just coming into town." He held in a chuckle

when she perked up and looked out the window, watching every building go by.

"There sure is a lot of graffiti in Italy," she said as the buildings slowed outside the window.

"Yeah," he admitted. "Back when I was a kid, they did a huge push to get rid of it all. It took less than a year for it to all look like this again." He motioned to the painted buildings.

"Still, it's all so different. I mean, you can't ride a bullet train from one city to another in the States. It took us two hours instead of three and we didn't have to drive."

He remembered her averseness to driving, especially when it snowed in the winter. To avoid it, she'd moved into a studio apartment downtown where she could easily walk everywhere. She still had a car, but most of the time, she walked wherever she was going or bummed rides from her friends.

"We're at the second stop," he said as the train slowed even more. "I had my cousin Dante make arrangements since the family technically owns one of the best hotels in the city."

"They do?" she asked, gasping.

"Yeah." He chuckled. "Damiano and Dante Cardone own a lot of businesses in Italy. New Edges, it's the family business. My cousin Dante took over running it a few years back, but they own a hell of a lot around here. Anyway, when I told him we were heading to Milan, he suggested a change in hotel. He said he took care of everything for us. Bumped us up to the presidential suite too." He grinned. "See, I told you having me tag along would be good."

She chuckled and leaned over to kiss him. "Just as long as you don't complain about all the shopping I'm going to do."

"I like shopping," he said as the train started moving again. "The hotel is near the shopping district. Or so my cousin tells me."

"So, Dante's father and your grandfather are brothers?" she asked, trying to figure out the family dynamics. She'd talked with Airlea briefly about it but was still confused.

"Yes, my grandfather and Dante's father are brothers. Their older sister, Florentina, is the black sheep in the family," he added. "The story goes that she hired men to kidnap Dante's older sister, Katie. You met her a few years back. Anyway, she hired men to kidnap her when it was discovered Katie was Damiano's daughter. Then she killed another man in the family's olive grove. She even tried to get rid of Airlea."

"What?" Claire gasped. "Why didn't Airlea tell me that juicy detail?"

He chuckled. "Airlea is... very forgiving." He shook his head. "My great-uncle hired her on as a nurse to help Dante get back on his feet when he was hit by the kidnappers while trying to save Katie."

"Wow, and you think I'm the one with bad luck. Your family is..." She motioned with her hands. "A hot mess."

He chuckled. "It's one of the reasons my parents are thankful that my grandfather moved to the States shortly after my father was born."

"Well, I'll have to contact Airlea and get all the details. She gave me her contact info at the wedding. I really liked talking with her."

"Dante mentioned that she'd said the same about you." He remembered his cousin's text message. He'd also told his cousin about the break-in and the theft.

Dante knew that Venice could be a hot spot for thieves, but two incidents in such a short time worried him as much as it worried Justin. His cousin suggested he keep Claire close by. It was another reason his cousin offered to put them up at his hotel. It was in the nicer part of the city.

Sure enough, as the train continued to travel into the city, the sides of the buildings became clean of graffiti.

"Wow, it's so beautiful here. I thought it was nice in Venice," she said as she turned away from the window. "It's a nice mix of old and new."

He nodded. He'd been to Milan twice before. Both trips had been long before he was a teenager. He could barely remember anything about the trips, other than he'd spent time with his cousins and distant relatives.

This time when the train slowed, they stepped off into the station.

"It feels strange not having luggage," she said as they walked through the train station. "Nice, but strange."

"All your toiletry items were in your backpack, right?" he asked as they walked past a pharmacy.

"Yes, the only things taken were my clothes and a couple things I'd purchased for my dad and Robin. I had the shot glasses shipped directly to my dad. So at least they didn't get those or the rest of the stuff I'd already shipped."

"Just your clothes then." He took her hand and stepped outside.

"At least the weather is nicer here." She lifted her face to the sunlight.

His breath caught in his throat just watching the sunlight hit her blonde hair as she relaxed.

"You're beautiful," he heard himself saying out loud.

She smiled and turned her face towards him. "Is this you trying to get out of shopping?"

He laughed and pulled her into his arms. "No, just... an observation." He kissed her.

"Come on, let's head towards the hotel. If there are some shops along the way, we can go in. Maybe we can buy something special for you to wear for dinner. Dante mentioned that the restaurant is one of the best in Milan. Of course, he'll say that about the place since he owns it, but still, I looked it up online and it's got over three hundred five-star reviews."

During the ten-block trip, they stopped at three shops, and Claire purchased clothing and a replacement suitcase just as bright as her last one. She purchased a couple pairs of jeans, several shirts, some sexy red and black underwear, and a sexy little black dress she claimed was for dinner that night.

"Every woman has to own at least one LBD," she had told him while she'd paid.

It took him a moment to realize that LBD stood for little black dress, and his mouth was watering at the thought of seeing her in the tight material.

They had just reached the block their hotel was on when he glanced up. Normally, he wouldn't have given the blond-haired guy walking towards them any of his attention, but the sheer size of him reminded him of the man that had taken Claire's suitcase in Venice.

When Justin locked eyes with him, it was as if something snapped. He knew without a doubt that it was the same man. The moment the man realized Justin knew, he sprinted towards them, pushing past a few people on the street and knocking down a woman holding a child's hand.

Justin only had a few seconds to step in front of Claire, shielding her behind his body before the man collided with them both.

Both of their feet flew out from under them as they fell

backwards. His body landed on top of Claire's, and he took the brunt of the man's bulk on his own.

The man recovered quickly and instead of grabbing Claire's new suitcase from where it had landed on the sidewalk beside them, he reached down and started pulling at Claire's backpack, which was wedged under the weight of both of their bodies.

Claire had screamed so loudly at the impact that two of the footmen from the hotel rushed towards them, blowing high-pitched whistles as they ran.

The larger man yanked his gaze from Claire's backpack to the two men rushing towards them and finally gave up and ran away.

"Are you okay?" one of the footmen asked him in English while the other snapped a few photos of the retreating man with his phone.

"Yes," he said, rolling off Claire. He ran his eyes over her to make sure she was okay, then helped her up. "Are you okay?" he asked her as he pulled her into his arms.

"Yes, I..." She pulled back and rubbed at her elbow and wrist. He gently took her arm in his hands and looked at her scraped skin. Both her elbow and palms had small cuts over her perfect skin.

"Is there a doctor..." Justin started to ask the footmen quickly.

"No," Claire shook her head. "It's just a scratch. I got worse the last time I went rock climbing with you." She shook some pebbles from her jeans. Then she stopped. "Was that..."

"The same man," he finished for her as he frowned at the crowded street where the man had disappeared moments before. "Yeah," he growled.

"Why?" Claire frowned up at him. "Why me?"

"I'm not sure." He turned back towards the two foot-men. One was on the phone, most likely to the police.

"We were just about to check in," he told the other man.

"We can wait for the police inside," he replied, motioning for them to follow him inside.

"He didn't want me. He wanted my bag," Claire said as they stepped inside and walked towards the front desk.

One of the footmen had walked with them to the front desk and quickly explained what had happened to the woman behind the counter. The clerk offered to call a doctor. Once again, Claire declined and said that she was fine.

"It's just a scratch." She sat down on one of the chairs near the desk while he checked them in.

The moment the clerk and the footmen realized that he was a Cardone, and related to the hotel's owner, they were almost swarmed with service. Not that they hadn't treated them nicely before, but now, all the employees were on their best behavior.

Drinks and food were offered. The clerk made a point to schedule private massages for them for later that evening, to help them recover from their ordeal.

Since he doubted Claire would pass up a free massage, he agreed to the appointments. Besides, that incident and the previous one that day had caused every single one of his muscles to tense.

Moments after they were checked in, the police showed up and they spent the next few moments reliving what had happened both outside and earlier that morning in Venice.

CHAPTER ELEVEN

Stepping into the suite in this hotel was like stepping into a modern art piece. The hotel was a great deal more modern than the place in Venice had been. It was more beautiful and much larger than she'd expected.

It was so large of a space that it included a kitchen and a dining room, which she supposed could be used as a conference area.

"Wow," Justin said, walking around after setting their bags down on the red leather sofas. The room was decorated in whites and creams, with the exception of the two bright sofas and a huge red splatter-art painting that hung over the marble fireplace.

"There's a balcony," Justin said, stepping through the large glass doors.

She followed him outside and admired the comfortable courtyard under some awnings. Small shrubbery and plants filled the sitting area, making it even more secluded. The view of the city was spectacular.

"Wow," she said, stopping beside him as they looked out over the more modern skyscape.

"When my cousin took over his father's business, he branched out into hotels," Justin said, glancing over at her. "It appears he went into the right business."

"I'd say. What now?" she asked, feeling slightly exhausted.

"How about we order room service, then head down for our free massages?"

"Free massages?" She perked up. He nodded and pulled her into his arms.

"Want to talk about what happened?" he asked.

She thought about it. "After I get something to eat," she said. "And shower."

"You head in, and I'll order us some grub," he said, and she followed him back inside.

Taking up her backpack and her new bag, she walked into the bedroom and was one again impressed with the beauty of the space. A huge king-sized bed with a tall cream-colored cushioned headboard sat in the middle of the room. An intricate glass chandelier hung over the bed. There were more glass doors heading out to the balcony, as well as a small sitting area.

Then she stepped into the bathroom and quite literally lost her breath.

"Justin?" she called out. "You've got to see this." She walked over to a glass and wood door as he rushed in, a concerned look on his face. "We have a steam room," she said as she opened the door.

"Wow." He chuckled. "Okay, I was thinking about hitting the pool, but now we may just chill out in here."

"This is amazing." She shut the door and then walked over to the massive private hot tub.

"There was one outside too," he said, motioning to the hot tub.

"Look at that shower," she gasped. She walked over to the glass door that surrounded the Italian marble shower that was easily bigger than the entire bathroom in her apartment. "What could anyone possibly do with all that space in here?"

His arms wrapped around her waist as he pulled her closer. "Later, we can find out." He kissed the top of her head.

She felt her knees go weak and relaxed back into his arms. "I'm thankful you're here," she said. She thought about handling everything that had happened on the trip herself.

He was silent for a moment then he placed his hands on her shoulders and turned her towards him. "Me too." He kissed her. "Take your shower. I'll order us some food." He kissed her again quickly, then left her alone.

She took a few moments to unpack her clothes and arrange her makeup and toiletry items in the bathroom drawers.

As she emptied her bag, she thought about what the man had hoped to steal from her. Why her? What did she have that he could possibly want?

She thought of her passport, her iPad, her cell phone. Nothing seemed out of the ordinary. There were so many other tourists that had what she did.

She turned on the shower and stepped in and let the hot water wash away all the aches and grime from the day. She lost herself in relaxing and when she opened her eyes and saw the dark figure standing on the other side of the foggy glass, she tensed.

"It's just me," Justin said quickly. "Our food is here."

"Oh." She reached up to turn on the water, but he

opened the door and stepped in beside her, his arms wrapping around her wet body.

"I thought I'd join you for a few minutes." He kissed her, and she once more relaxed completely.

She enjoyed the feeling of his muscular body next to hers. Then his hands started to roam over her hips and up to her ribs. He cupped her breasts, and she moaned his name. There was more passion in the kiss than any that had come before. More urgency, more desire than she'd ever experienced before.

"Tell me how much you want me to continue touching you?" he said in a low tone.

"Yes, please," she begged, reaching for him. When she wrapped her fingers around his length, this time it was his turn to moan.

"I need you," he said into her wet hair. "Now." He growled again as he nudged her back against the marble wall. His fingers dug into her hip as he lifted her leg, wrapping it around his hips as he plunged into her.

She held onto him, tears forming in her eyes at how he made her feel wanted, desired, loved. No one had ever treated her quite like Justin had. Even before they'd crossed from friendship into whatever this was. Lust? Love?

For this moment, she didn't care. All that mattered was enjoying this moment. The feeling of him inside her, of his hands on her. Of his kisses weakening every fiber of her being. For now, all that mattered was him.

After the shower, they got dressed, her in a pair of yoga pants and a tank top that she'd had in her backpack, him in a pair of gym shorts and a T-shirt. Then they stepped out onto the patio and ate lunch with the muffled sounds of the city far below them.

It was only after she'd finished half her soup and sandwich that he brought up the attacks.

"What did you do before I ran into you in Venice?" he asked her.

"Before?" She thought about it. "Shopped. Ate at a few restaurants. Had a lot of gelato." She smiled. "That's about it." She shrugged and pushed her plate aside.

"You didn't talk to anyone?" he asked as he finished sipping on the beer he'd ordered.

"I mean, sure, but nothing out of the ordinary."

"What did you buy?"

She thought about it. "Everything I purchased, I shipped home right before I saw you outside my hotel."

"Still, humor me. What did you purchase?" He pushed his own plate aside.

"Some scarfs, some material I planned on making a skirt with when I returned home, a mask, some key chains and Venice trinkets." She ticked off the items. "I have pictures of some." She pulled out her phone and opened her pictures to the items. She handed it to him.

"Where is this?" he asked, showing her a picture of the mask shop.

"Some little mask shop down a back alley." She shrugged. "I purchased this one." She swiped the image and showed him the mask she'd purchased.

"Who is this?" he asked with a frown.

She looked at the image and shrugged. "The store worker I guess." She frowned. "Why?"

"Hang on." He set her phone down and then walked inside. Moments later, he brought out his computer and set it down. She waited while he searched. Then he took her phone and held the picture she'd taken up to his screen. He turned the screens towards her.

She held in a gasp. There on his computer was a news article from a Venetian paper about a missing man. The guy in the picture could easily be the man in her photo.

"Do you think it's the same guy?" she asked.

Justin turned the computer back towards him and translated the story for her.

"Gabriele Lombardi was reported missing by his brother Marco late Tuesday evening. Gabriele was manning the family shop, Arte allo stato puro." Justin glanced up at her. "An authentic Venetian mask shop." He sighed as he looked back down at the article. "When Marco returned to the shop after running a quick errand, the shop was empty. His brother hasn't been heard from since. Any information about Gabriele's whereabouts will be met with a reward," Justin finished up.

"Okay, so the shop owner's brother went missing after I left." She was silent for a moment. "Should we contact the police? Call this number?"

He looked at the article again. "Maybe. You're probably the last one to see him." He frowned. "Is there anything you can tell the police? Was anyone else in the shop?"

"No." She frowned as she thought back. "He said he was closed." She closed her eyes as she played back what had happened. "He seemed edgy. As if he was waiting..." She remembered him calling her the American. She'd believed it was just her translation, but now she wasn't so sure. "He asked me if I was the American."

"The American?" Justin asked and she nodded.

"I thought I was just misunderstanding him. That maybe my translation skills weren't as good. Or his English wasn't, when he said it in English too. But now with this." She motioned to the screen.

"You just purchased the mask?" he asked, taking her phone, and looking at the image again.

"Yes. I shipped it along with the rest of the stuff to my place. It'll arrive in a few days." She shrugged. "I can track the package?" She motioned to his computer.

He pushed his computer towards her. She took her phone and went to the website for the shipping company then searched her tracking number.

"It hasn't shipped yet." She sighed. "I knew I should have paid for the faster service. It's probably still in Venice."

"Can you change the address to here?" he asked.

"I can try." She frowned. "You'll have to translate..." He leaned closer and between them they managed to pay for the faster shipping and change the address to their hotel.

"The box of items will be here the day after tomorrow." She leaned back with a smile. "So now we can get to the bottom of things."

"Since we handled that, how about we head down and get those massages?" he offered.

"Sounds wonderful. Think they'll have some champagne for us?" she asked.

He chuckled. "I'd bet on it."

She'd never paid to have a message before, so she wasn't sure what to expect. When they stepped into the spa, she was a little overwhelmed and felt seriously underdressed.

The employees all wore white outfits, and their hair and makeup were perfect. The spa was just as impressive as the rest of the hotel.

They were led past the reception desk, through a softly lit room and into a larger room.

"Couples massages," Justin said to her after the woman spoke to him in Italian. That much she'd gathered. Still, it was nice to have him translate. "We can change in here," he said when they were left alone in the changing room. "Here." He handed her a robe. "Strip down." He took his own robe.

"Have you ever had a massage before?" she asked, feeling slightly embarrassed about getting completely naked. Then she thought about him being naked and having the pretty brunette who had showed them in running her hands all over him.

Justin chuckled, gaining her attention. "I've had a few, but never one for couples. This will be a first. You?" She shook her head. "Trust me, no one will see all of you. If you want, leave your underwear on," he said, stepping out of his boxer shorts.

"What about you?" she asked as he wrapped the robe around himself.

"I'll be covered with a towel. They don't set out to see all your fun bits." He winked.

"Right." She sighed.

"Plus, we'll be in our own private room. Not the message chairs we walked by. Those are only for walk-in back massages. We've got the whole package." He finished. "Go on." He motioned to her, then stood back and waited until she stripped off everything except for her panties.

When they stepped into their private room, a bottle of champagne was chilling and they were each handed a glass. She took a large sip before lying down on the table.

She jumped slightly when the masseuse's hands started working on her. Five minutes later, she was fast asleep and completely relaxed.

CHAPTER TWELVE

J ustin had to admit that, even after what they'd gone through that morning, the evening was shaping up to be more perfect than any he'd had before. After their massages, they headed back upstairs for a two-hour nap.

When they woke, they showered and dressed. He wore the best pants he had packed and a button-up shirt, which he had to iron, and Claire wore the new sexy black dress she'd purchased.

The moment she stepped out of the bathroom wearing the dress, so many memories of her wearing similar clothing in the past surfaced. Only this time, she had dressed with spending the evening with him in mind.

"You look amazing," he said easily, pulling her into his arms.

"You're not so bad either." She chuckled. "For some reason, I'm starving."

"Me too. Let's head downstairs." He took her hand and they started downstairs.

The staff had assured them that the presidential suites floor couldn't be accessed by any other guests unless they had special key cards. There were four such suites on the top floor and, according to the clerk who had checked them in, the other three rooms would remain empty the entire duration of their stay. Dante had apparently arranged it after their last conversation about their break-in at the other hotel.

When they were seated in the main dining room, he ordered a bottle of wine as she glanced over the menu.

"Dante says they have the best steaks here," he suggested.

Claire glanced over the menu at him. "We're in Italy. Isn't it some sort of rule that we have to eat Italian?"

He chuckled. "Do you think the Italians don't eat beef?"

She set her menu down and sighed. "Sure. Meatballs and sausages."

He laughed. "Okay." He slid her menu away from her. "Be prepared to be amazed."

Without looking at his menu, he ordered her a dish of beef braciole and a house steak for himself, knowing they would share. He added a few different authentic Italian appetizers, some that he knew she'd probably never tried before.

"You know, when you come into our restaurant, you can try more than just the lasagna," he said once the waitress left them alone.

"Why would I?" She leaned a little closer on the table. "Your father's lasagna is the best. I've had dreams about it." When he chuckled, she continued. "No, for real. That summer your dad was out for surgery..."

"He tore a ligament in his elbow," he remembered.

"Right, and your mother took over the kitchen." She shook her head. "It just wasn't the same. Then he was back and the first day I ordered two helpings." She smiled. "Tell me you're able to repeat his recipe?"

He nodded. "My mother makes it like her family, my father like his. I can make both versions," he added with a smile.

"Nothing against your mother's family, but your dad's side of the family has won my vote," she said, sipping her wine.

When the food arrived, they were both once again very relaxed. The appetizers were a huge hit with Claire, who vowed to expand the selections she chose at his restaurant when she returned home.

He watched her very closely as she tried the beef rolls and saw the moment she fell in love with the food.

"Here, try this." He held up a forkful of his steak. She scooped up some of her food and held it out for him to try.

"Wow, that's as good as this." She motioned between their plates.

"Told you," he said with a smile.

For the next hour, they ate, drank, and flirted with one another as if they were on their first date. In truth, it was probably their thousandth dinner together. It wasn't even their first dinner on this trip.

Somehow, tonight seemed more special. Maybe because he'd changed his travel plans and had committed to going along with her? Maybe it was the danger of earlier that day? Whatever the reason, he wanted to enjoy every moment he could that evening.

"What are the plans for tomorrow?" he asked her as they rode the elevator back up to their rooms. He'd arranged for a bottle of champagne and desserts to be delivered to their room. He'd planned on sitting outside on the balcony and enjoying them with Claire while enjoying the night lights of the city.

He knew that Claire was a little tipsy. Hell, the wine had gone to his head as well. When they stepped off the elevator, holding onto one another, a waiter was already waiting for them outside their door.

After the woman rolled the cart inside, he tipped her and shut and locked the door.

"What do you say we take this outside on the balcony for some fresh air?" he suggested.

Instead, Claire took his hand and lifted it to cover her breast. "After," she said softly before kissing him.

It was strange how much power she had over him. With a flutter of her eyelashes, a lick of her lips, a simple touch, his mind went completely blank and the desire for her outweighed everything else.

"You have this power," he said between kisses. "Do you know how much power you hold over me?" He hiked up the skirt of her dress as his hands roamed over the soft skin of her thighs.

As a response, she moaned and buried her fingers into his hair, pulling him down for a deeper kiss.

Being with Claire was like touching a live wire. Every single one of his nerve endings ignited and sparked to fire, burning hotter than anything he'd felt in his entire life.

They made it to the sofa. Her dress and that sexy black underwear ended up in a pile on the floor along with all of his clothes.

When he could think straight again, his breathing labored, beads of sweat rolling down his back, he realized that he'd forgotten to use a condom this time.

"Claire," he groaned. "You had me so turned around that I forgot..."

"I know," she said, somehow sounding happy. He leaned up and looked down at her. "I've been on the pill since I was eighteen," she said with a shrug. "I'm clean."

"I am too." He frowned. "I wasn't..." He shook his head. "Not that it would be such a bad thing." He tilted his head. "Kids, that is."

She laughed. "You're as dimwitted after sex as you are in the morning."

He chuckled. "Okay." He took her wrists and pinned her hands above her head. "That's fighting dirty."

She wrapped her legs around his hips and held onto him. "Who ever said I fight fair? You've known me my entire life. Have I ever fought fair?"

She twisted and he allowed her to push him down on the sofa as he laughed. Once she had him pinned down, his hands high above his own head, she leaned down and ran her lips over him.

"This time, I'm in charge," she purred, and he leaned back to allow her to take over.

By the time they made it out to the patio with their desserts, they had both changed into sweats. There was a gas firepit and even though it was warm out, he turned it on as they sipped their cold champagne and enjoyed the rich chocolate mousse dessert.

"This is much nicer than anything I'd ever hoped for," she said with a slight yawn.

"I'm glad I changed up my plans."

She glanced up at him. "What plans?" she joked.

He shrugged. "I had some."

"Oh?" She shifted and looked at him. "For the past five years, you've been working."

"And going to school," he added.

She frowned at him. "You have?"

He laughed. "Why do you think I've been working so hard? I've been paying for online business classes."

"Business?" She tucked her free leg under herself and tilted her head as she ran her eyes over him. "You have?"

He nodded. "It was my dad's idea. A good one, but don't tell him that," he joked.

"Business?" she asked again.

He sighed. "My father thinks that if I'm going to take over the family business, I should know how to run it. It's actually given me a lot of great ideas. Like expansion."

"I should have taken classes," she said with a frown.

"You did for a while," he reminded her.

"Yeah, but I grew bored and flunked out. My heart just wasn't in it. I want to be doing, not learning about how to do."

He laughed. "You can't be successful at doing if you don't know how."

"That's not necessarily true. There are loads of successful businesspeople out there that have no degrees."

"True," he agreed. "But for me, school has helped."

She nudged his shoulder. "Not everyone can be as awesome as me."

He laughed and wrapped his arm around her, pulling her back down to his side. "That's true too." He kissed the top of her head.

"It's a perfect night," she said with a sigh as they looked into the flames.

"It is." He felt his heart swell.

"I'm glad you're here," she said again.

"Me too. So, tomorrow?"

She chuckled. "More shopping. There are a few shops from some of my favorite designers that I want to go visit."

He held in a groan. After all, he'd agreed to the trip

knowing full well what her intentions were. He knew what shopping with Claire was like. He'd been stuck going with her more than once in his life. It wasn't just shopping with her, but any woman. Once, his mother had taken him to the mall before Christmas, and he'd purposely gotten lost so he could sneak off to play laser tag. When his mother had found him at the cinnamon roll place, she'd assumed he'd found his way towards the smells and had purchased him a large sticky bun. What she hadn't known is that he'd used some of his saved tip money and had already had one before she'd found him. Still, he'd been ten and had easily wolfed down the bonus sugary treat.

"I can hear you complaining internally," she said, breaking his thoughts.

"Just wondering if there are any places where I can get some cinnamon rolls tomorrow," he joked.

Her eyes narrowed at him. "You are not going to get lost again, are you?"

He sighed. "You know me too well." He smiled as he pulled her back in for another kiss.

CHAPTER THIRTEEN

The following day, they explored Milan completely. She hit every shop, boutique, and fabric store she'd marked on her travel list with Justin by her side.

There were several times that he actually looked like he was enjoying himself. As payment, she located what was said to be the best bakery in the city to reward him with some of the best cinnamon buns she'd ever had. They had plans to return to the bakery and even marked it on the map app, so they knew the quickest route.

Since she had purchased a new suitcase, she had plenty of room for the new items. Still, they stopped and shipped home a box of souvenirs they had purchased. Justin had a few items for his parents that he included in her things as well.

The following day, they hung around the hotel while waiting for the package to arrive. First, they ordered room service, followed by a quick swim in the pool. Okay, most of their time was spent in the hot tub. Justin claimed his feet were sore from all the walking the day before. Her smart watch had clocked them walking over eleven miles.

They followed the swim with a light lunch down in the bar area and were informed shortly after that her package had arrived.

"Do you really think there's something in here that will help figure out what happened to Gabriele Lombardi?" she asked as he carried the box into their rooms.

"Who knows, but if there isn't then we need to figure out why that man has attacked us twice now." He set the box down.

She watched as he opened the box, setting each of the items she'd purchased down on the table until he reached the box that held the mask.

"That's it," she said.

"Did you wrap it yourself?" he asked, looking at the brown paper wrapping around the box.

"No, he went to the back and wrapped it. Since it was done so well, I figured it was better not to open it and just ship it that way." She stood next to him as they both looked down at the box.

"Here goes." He removed the tape and carefully opened the box, as if it was a bomb instead of a mask tucked inside.

She didn't know what she'd expected. They both stood over the opened box, holding their breath.

The mask sat perfectly tucked in a cocoon of newspapers.

"It's... cute." He lifted the mask and turned it over. He set the mask down and dug through the papers. "It's... just the mask."

She picked up the mask and looked at it. It was the mask she'd requested but she scanned the face a little more closely and noticed a difference. "This isn't the same mask that I purchased," she said with a frown. "There's a teardrop here." She motioned to the area. "Mine didn't have it."

He was quiet for a moment. "Let me see your picture." When she handed him her phone, he compared the two. "It looks like the same one. But you're right, they are identical except this." He tapped the stone, which instantly fell off into his fingers. "Oops." He held it out as he looked up at her. "Sorry."

"It's okay." She smiled. "I didn't like it there anyway."

He handed her the gem and then zoomed into the area on her photo. It definitely hadn't been there in her pictures. "Okay." He picked up the mask and turned it over. "So, they aren't the same masks. What else is different?"

She put the gem into her pocket and then picked up the mask. "This mask appears a lot older than the other." She turned it over. Inside, there was a thin layer of material near the top of the jester fringes. "This is different." She motioned to the area as she handed it back to him.

Justin set it on the table and then looked at her. "Is it okay if I..." he asked, and she nodded.

"Do what you have to." She motioned. "I think getting to the bottom of this is more important than keeping the mask intact at this point. We've already lost the gem."

He set the mask down and walked into the kitchen where he rummaged through the drawers. When he returned, he held a kitchen knife. He sat down, placing the mask directly in front of him.

She watched for the next few moments as he carefully peeled back the material.

"What?" she asked when he pulled out a small piece of paper.

"It appears to be a cipher," he said after looking at the numbers and letters. "Like a code." He set the thin piece of paper down. The ink was dark, but the paper appeared well worn and almost see through.

"Like in the spy movies?" she asked, her ears ringing as her head starting to spin. "Why is it in my mask?"

"Good question." He set the paper down. "So, what do we know? We know that Gabriele Lombardi went missing after he gave you this mask."

"He called me the American," she reminded him.

"Right, as in... he was expecting the person to pick this up to be from the States."

"Right," she agreed, then she gasped when she remembered something. "I bumped into a woman leaving the shop."

"A woman?" he asked. "Who? Did you see her?"

She shrugged. "I was too excited about getting the mask. I don't even think I looked up," she admitted.

He sighed. "Okay, so whoever it was that should have picked this up was an American woman." He rolled his shoulders as she watched.

"That doesn't give us a lot to go on. Do you know how many American women I bumped into during my few days in Venice?" she asked.

He nodded. "Yeah, probably hundreds." He turned towards her. "What we do know is that whoever it was that was trying to get this not only made Gabriele Lombardi disappear but knows who you are since she's sent her goon after you twice now."

"Three times," she corrected. "If you count the break-in."

His eyes widened. "Right." He glanced towards the doors. "And they know right where we are staying now." He looked down at the mask. "And know we have what they want."

Claire felt her stomach roll, her head spin, and her vision gray. Justin's calm voice broke her from the spell.

"Hey," he said, pulling her into his arms. "I'm right here. They're not going to get to us again. I promise."

"How can you be so sure?" she asked as she listened to his heartbeat.

"Because we're not going to give them the chance."

"Are we going to call the police?"

He was quiet for a moment. "No, even better. We're going to call my family."

He dropped his hold on her and pulled out his cell phone.

She listened for the next twenty minutes while he talked to Dante. The fact that he so easily went between English and Italian baffled and impressed her.

When he hung up, she waited as he paced the room.

"So?" she asked him, growing impatient. "What does he suggest?"

"A change of plans."

She'd gathered that much. So much for her visit to Florence and Rome.

"And?" she asked.

"We're going to stay here for another few days, since it's safe enough. After which, we'll head down to visit my family."

"At the olive grove?" she asked, eager.

Justin nodded. "If it's okay with you."

"Hell, yes, it is," she said quickly. "Ever since Airlea talked about the place, I've wanted to go."

"Then it's settled. We head there in two days. Until then, we're supposed to stick as close to the hotel as possible. This"—he tapped the mask as he put the cipher back in place— "is going to be locked up in the safe."

"The hotel one in the closet? Will it be safe enough?" she asked.

"No." He smiled. "Dante has provided us with another option." He walked back into the living room and slid one of the red chairs aside. He pulled back the carpet and part of the floor. A safe sat directly underneath. He punched in a code and then slid the mask inside it before locking it up and putting the flooring and the chair back. "There. Only four people know of the safe's existence, and three of their last names are Cardone. The manager, who is on her way up here now, is the fourth. Dante trusts her completely."

"Good to know," she said easily. "What about the rest of the stuff?"

"We ship it home, like the rest." He put everything back in the box. "Dante has arranged for it to be picked up and sent for us." There was a knock on the door and Justin smiled. "I'll hand it to my cousin; he knows how to get things done."

Justin walked over and met the woman standing outside their door.

"Hello, Mr. Cardone, I'm Gina, manager of the Astori. Mr. Cardone called and said that you had an important package to be shipped out?" the woman said in English.

"Yes," Justin said, handing her the box. "The address is…"—he motioned to the first shipping label— "this one."

"Perfect." Gina nodded. "I'll see that it's done myself."

"Thank you," Justin said before shutting the door again. "There, that's handled. Now how about we take a nap?"

She laughed. "I'm on vacation. Sleep is for when we're home." She looked outside. "There are more than a dozen things still on my list to do in town." She frowned. "But if it's not safe…"

"What sort of things?"

"Tourist things," she said, pulling up her agenda.

He scrolled through them while she waited. "A few of

these are questionable, even if we didn't have someone after the mask." He shook his head. "But some should be okay during the daylight." He glanced out. "We have a few more hours left. How about we hit Duomo di Milano today since it's fairly close by and take a shuttle to the others in the morning? In the meantime, Dante is going to have his staff watching our rooms very closely."

Seeing the Duomo di Milano was at the top of her list anyway, so she agreed. After shopping, the tourist trap places were a perk. Thankfully, she'd been able to hit all of the shops that she'd wanted to see. Or so she'd thought.

As they walked to the massive cathedral, she strolled through a few more shops along the way. She picked up a few more items, this time keeping in mind how much room she had left in her new luggage.

Strolling around the six-hundred-year-old cathedral, she realized just how short life was. She wondered if there had been Cardones around when the structure had been built.

When she asked Justin, he just laughed and said probably.

Did she even know her own family history beyond her grandparents on her father's side? Her mother's family had never really been around. Her dad's parents lived a few miles down the road. She saw them more than she saw her father most days.

Their parents had been from Wyoming, or so they'd told her once when she'd had to do a report back in middle school. She didn't know much more about them.

"It must be nice, knowing just where your family came from," she said as they strolled back towards their hotel.

"How so?" He glanced down at her. "It's not like it affects my day-to-day life."

"No, I suppose it doesn't. Still, you know who they are. I

only have my dad, sister, and grandparents. You have a slew of cousins, uncles, and... what are Dante and Airlea's kids to you?"

He laughed. "Third cousins once removed, I think." He shrugged. "That doesn't even account for Dante's sister and her half-brother's family." He shook his head. "My family is too big, if you ask me."

She wrapped her arm in his. "I like all of them that I've met so far."

"How about some gelato?" He nodded towards a shop.

"You read my mind," she joked as they strolled inside. "I'm going to have to diet when I get back, but it'll be so worth it."

This time, they sat in the bright lights of the little shop, enjoying the cold treat along with a handful of other people.

The fact that there were so many memories of her and Justin hanging out just like this had her smiling. She loved that she knew so much about him. Loved that he knew so much about her. Their friendship meant more to her than any other friendships she had.

"This is nice." He leaned back in his chair. "My parents never allowed me to eat this much gelato. Ever." He smiled. "I'm seriously thinking we need to offer more flavors ourselves."

"I like the flavors you have, but it wouldn't hurt to offer this." She held up her dulce de leche gelato.

He laughed. "Agreed." He stilled, and his eyes locked with hers. "This is nice," he said again, only this time she knew he wasn't talking about the iced treat.

"Yes." She swallowed the lump in her throat. "It is."

CHAPTER FOURTEEN

Justin stayed vigilant as they spent the next couple of days roaming the city. He was constantly scanning the crowds for the man that had attacked them.

So far, they'd enjoyed themselves exploring Milan. They spent more time shopping than he personally would have liked, but just being with Claire was reward enough.

They tried several different restaurants, and there were a few classical dishes that he thought about adding to their own menu when he returned.

"You're quiet," she said as they sat out on the balcony, watching the sunset on their fourth and last evening in Milan. They were dressed and ready to head downstairs for dinner, but still had almost half an hour before their reservation time.

Claire was wearing another one of her new dresses, this one in a soft blue material that clung to her and had spaghetti straps. Her shorter hair was curled in one of his favorite styles she wore.

The last week with Claire had been by far the best time in his life. He never wanted it to end. He worried that things would change when they returned home. That their relationship would change back to what it had been all of their lives.

He wrapped his arms around her and held on as the sky darkened.

"I'm thinking about us." He rested his chin on her head. He felt the moment she tensed.

"And?" she asked after a moment.

He sighed. "And I'm being selfish. I don't want this time to end."

She relaxed in his arms. "Me either." She turned and wrapped her arms around him. "Promise me that nothing will change between us when we get home."

"I'd love to make that promise, but..." He leaned back and looked down into her eyes. "Home equals complications. My parents, your dad, your grandparents, all of our friends." He listed things off that had started running through his mind in the past few days. "Not to mentions our jobs."

"I don't see anything there that would change the way we feel about each other. Do you?" she asked.

He smiled. "No." Leaning down, he brushed his lips across hers. "Not the way we feel. Maybe some of the time we're able to spend together. But nothing could get in the way of how I feel about you." He kissed her again.

"We'd better head downstairs. We wouldn't want to miss our reservation time. They said tonight was going to be packed."

"It's a weekend." He shrugged and took her hand and led her through their room.

When they stepped into the restaurant, they realized just how crowded the place could get.

"I guess it was a good thing we made reservations," Claire said as they waited in line to check in.

"Claire?" someone said from behind them.

They both turned around to see Madison Hayes strolling towards them. The woman was wearing a very tight, very short black skirt with a hot pink suit jacket with nothing underneath. Somehow her breasts miraculously stayed covered by the material. She glided on four-inch heels as if they were tennis shoes. Her long black hair had been straightened and hung over her shoulders.

The closer she got to them; the more tense he could feel Claire become.

"What luck," Madison said easily as she walked up, and air-kissed Claire then turned to him. "Justin, you're here too." She air-kissed him. "I thought you were heading home after Venice."

"Change of plans," he said, taking Claire's arm.

"I knew there was something between the two of you." Her smile grew. "Just friends." She shook her head, sending her long hair flowing around her. "What are you doing at the Astori?" She waved to the crowd.

"Justin's family owns the hotel," Claire said as the line moved forwards.

"What fun," Madison purred. "Oh!" She snapped her fingers as if she'd just remembered. "That's right. You're a Cardone."

He nodded, and the uneasy feeling in his gut grew. Madison knew exactly who he was. After all, he'd been introduced to her at the wedding as Isabella's cousin. How many times had she made mention of him being related to Dante? And he and Claire had sat with Dante and Airlea during the entire dinner.

"What are you doing in Milan?" Claire asked.

"Oh." Madison waved her hand as if shooing a fly. "When you mentioned that you were heading here, I thought it would be fun to pop over here for some summer shopping. I simply must have a new summer wardrobe."

Just then they were called to the front of the line, and Justin explained that they had reservations.

"Oh, that was smart, making reservations." She glanced at them. "Any chance you have room for one more?"

"I'm sorry, miss," the maître d' broke in. "The reservation is for a table of two."

"Oh well." Madison shifted her gaze to the man. "Surely you can make room. After all,"—she leaned against Justin's arm as if they were old friends— "this is the owner's cousin."

The maître d' glanced at him, and he must have seen the uncomfortableness in Justin's face before he replied.

"On any other night, yes, we'd have room. But as it is, I'm sorry. If Mr. Cardone wishes, room service can be…"

"No," Justin broke in. "Thank you, we'll dine here." He turned to Madison. "Maybe next time." He took Claire's hand as a dark look crossed Madison's eyes and her lips thinned slightly. "It was nice bumping into you." He motioned for the man to show them to their table.

As the man handed him his menu after helping Claire to sit down, Justin said to him, "Thank you for that." The man nodded and disappeared.

"What do you think she's doing here?" Claire asked when they were alone.

"Good question. I heard from my cousin's husband that Madison's reputation as a spoiled socialite diva is dead on. Maybe it's just as she said." He shrugged. "She's shopping?"

Claire frowned as she glanced towards the door. Since

his back was to the area, he leaned closer and asked. "Is she still there?"

Claire shook her head slightly. "No." She leaned to the right a little. "I don't see her in line anymore either."

"Maybe she was humiliated that she couldn't get in?" he asked.

"She didn't look humiliated. She looked pissed," Claire said, and he saw her visibly shiver.

"Cold?" he asked her.

"No, just... That feeling you get when you realize that you've just made an enemy. Something tells me that her interest in me has been a scheme since the beginning."

He turned his head and glanced towards the door and thought about looking into Madison Hayes himself later that night.

"Let's forget about her and try to enjoy our last night here." He took her hand in his.

"That sounds like a good idea." Claire smiled, but he could see the uncertainty in her eyes.

All through dinner, the conversation remained light but the exchange with Madison had put a strain on both of their minds.

Dinner was wonderful, as he'd come to expect from his cousin's place. So far, they hadn't had one bad meal.

"I'm stuffed," Claire said, leaning back in her chair as she sipped her wine.

"Too full for some dessert?"

She smiled. "No one is ever too full for dessert. Just... maybe a walk first? Then we can order something in our rooms or maybe get something while we're out?"

"Sounds like a plan." He was just about to ask for the check when Gina started heading their way. The manager appeared shaken, which was one of the reason's she'd caught his attention.

"Mr. Cardone, Miss Stein." She cleared her throat. "I'm sorry to bother you, but there's been an incident."

Just then their server appeared. "Is there a problem?" the woman asked Gina.

"No." Gina turned to the waitress. "I'll be taking care of their bill tonight." She waved the woman away. "If you would please follow me to my office?"

He wanted to ask what the problem was but figured she didn't want to cause a scene in front of the other patrons.

Instead, he helped Claire up from the table and they followed her in silence out of the restaurant and down a side hallway into what he assumed was her office.

"Please." Gina motioned them to sit. "The police will be here shortly to talk to you. But until then, I can assure you that we are looking into the situation completely."

"What's happened?" Claire asked, worry filling her eyes.

"It appears that someone gained access to your rooms," Gina said with a frown.

"How?" he asked, understanding that the dread and concern on Gina's face wouldn't be so deep for a mere break-in.

"Someone attacked one of my staff and forced her to give them access to the penthouse floor," Gina answered.

"Oh no," Claire gasped. "Is your staff member, okay?"

Gina sighed. "No." She closed her eyes. "Raita is being rushed to the hospital as we speak. She has worked for the Astori for more than five years."

"What happened?" Claire asked, leaning forward slightly.

"She's been shot," Gina answered just as a knock

sounded on her door. "That will be the police." She stood up and walked over to open the door.

Two officers in black stepped into the room. One was a female with straight dark hair, the other an older balding man.

Before they could speak, Justin turned to Gina and asked. "Did they find the safe?"

Gina smiled slightly. "No, it appears not. Your package is still safe."

"Thank you." He turned to talk with the police.

Since they had been busy in the restaurant, they didn't have to do much explaining as to their whereabouts when the shooting took place. What they did have to was once again go through the items in their rooms and see if anything had been taken.

He waited to check the safe until after the officers had left. Gina agreed to move them to another presidential suite at the end of the hall, since there was cleaning that needed to be done in their current rooms.

Once they were alone, he collected the mask from the safe. He tucked it into his backpack, helped Claire gather her things, and hauled everything to their new rooms.

Since they would be heading out in the morning, he didn't even unpack his things from his backpack. Instead, he and Claire climbed into the bed and fell fast asleep, holding onto one another.

When they woke, they lay in bed for a while, talking.

"Do you think Raita is okay?" Claire asked him.

"We can check before we head out," he suggested.

"It's strange..." she started, then stopped.

"What?" He glanced down at her. She was resting her chin on his chest as she looked out the windows. This suite wasn't as nice or as big as the last one, but still, the row of windows allowed in the sunlight.

She leaned up, resting her chin on her fist, which rested on his chest. "It's just too much of a coincidence that Madison showed up here the night someone broke into our hotel. We were with her that night in Venice too, when someone broke into our rooms."

He thought about it, then nodded. "Yeah, we were. What are you saying?"

She titled her head. "She is an American woman." He waited, then Claire sat up, crossed her legs, and held up her fingers. "She was in Venice. She showed extreme interest in me from the moment she saw me. Maybe I didn't see whoever I bumped into outside the mask shop, but maybe she saw me? Besides, she was constantly asking me about my trip." She kept ticking off her fingers. "Not to mention that she was with us the night our hotel was broken into. Then, she shows up here and, bam, our rooms are broken into again." Claire's eyes narrowed. "I believe in coincidences, but this many?" She shook her head. "Besides, your cousin's husband said it himself. She's a bored socialite. Maybe whatever the cipher says, maybe it's something to do with her?"

He thought about it for a moment and realized that Claire's theory was just as likely as any he'd run through his head. He grabbed his laptop and, for the next hour while they waited for room service, they researched Madison Hayes.

CHAPTER FIFTEEN

Maybe she was way off. The more they looked into Madison, the more Claire realized that the woman was nothing more than a social butterfly. Well, maybe not a butterfly. More like a dragonfly. The woman was always jet setting off to somewhere exotic in one of her family's private planes or one of the three massive yachts.

Madison had been telling the truth at least about why she was in Milan. She'd posted several pictures of her with at least one high-profile designer yesterday before they'd run into her outside the restaurant.

And she'd posted a short video explaining why she'd simply had to come to Milan after Venice after bumping into Claire. The fact that she'd mentioned Claire by name caused a boulder to settle in Claire's stomach.

"Maybe we're wrong?" Claire said to Justin over breakfast.

"About Madison?" he asked, sipping his second cup of coffee. She nodded as she set her phone down. She'd been scrolling through Madison's social media feeds. "Why do you say that?" he asked.

"Because there's nothing here. Before she bumped into us last night, she'd posted about coming to Milan. Not once, but four times. Someone who posts about it beforehand... doesn't that discount their sneakiness? After all, she told the whole world she was coming."

"If she was some sort of mastermind, that would track," he offered.

"You really think that someone like her would risk her life for whatever the cipher is?" She picked up her phone and showed him a picture of Madison sipping tea on the veranda of a château in Venice while wearing nothing but a robe that had slipped dangerously low on her shoulders, exposing her perfect double Ds.

Justin thought about it for a moment before turning his computer screen around. "What do you see?" He motioned to a few pictures of Madison. Each one showed her perfectly posed, wearing either close to nothing or expensive designer clothing. Every single one was taken in some beautiful place, or she was standing next to an expensive car, boat, or plane. "I see someone who likes attention," Justin said. "Someone who is very narcissistic." He clicked the mouse pad and the images changed to a row of pictures of Madison holding expensive guns, posed at a gun range, or lying in a bed of shiny weapons. "An attention seeker. Several of her posts are extremely controversial in nature, then she pounces on anyone who comments, no matter which side they've taken." He scrolled through her social media and then turned it around. "She posts things that are borderline sexist." He motioned to one post. The image attached to it was of her standing in stilettos and an evening gown while a white male waiter in a tuxedo held out a tray of cash to her. Madison looked bored and uninterested, as if passing up a glass of champagne instead of thousands if not hundreds of thousands of dollars. He turned the screen back to himself. "The post reads, 'The only thing a man is good for. Delivering the goods.' Many of her followers liked the post, but there were dozens of comments voicing outrage. Almost every single one Madison responded to with even more hate. She lives for attention. Lives for conflict."

Claire smiled. "You really should have been a psychologist."

He chuckled. "Maybe I will." He motioned to the screen. "One thing is clear. She's either a stupid person who likes attention, or she's extremely smart and knows how to cover her tracks. Whatever is in that cipher is worth killing over." He clicked the computer mouse again and then turned the screen towards her. It was a news article in Italian. The headline read, "Body of Gabriele Lombardi discovered in canal."

Claire's stomach rolled as she looked at the image of the man who had helped her that day in the mask shop.

"Do you really think that Madison could kill someone and then toss his body in a canal?" she asked Justin.

He shrugged. "I guess it all depends on what secrets the cipher holds."

Claire's eyes moved to Justin's backpack where he'd put the mask late last night.

"What do we do now?" she asked.

He smiled. "Now, we put all this away, shower, pack up, and head to my family's place."

"Shouldn't we tell the police what we know?" she asked.

"What do we know? You were in the shop, purchased a

mask, and Gabriele Lombardi was still alive. You thought you bumped into a woman on the way out, but you can't remember even the smallest detail. Claire, I hate to say this, but it doesn't look good for you." He took her hand in his. "If we had any actual facts to tell the police, we'd tell them. As it is, last night, we pretty much told them everything we know, and even then, we had to defend ourselves. Thankfully, we'd been downstairs in a room full of dozens of guests and employees as our alibi witnesses. For now, let's hold off."

She knew what he was saying was true. Last night some of the questions from the police had made her feel as if she was on trial instead of a victim of the crime.

They showered in a shower much like the one in their old room, except that this bathroom didn't have the sauna, which they had used and enjoyed almost every evening. This room was also missing the private courtyard balcony, which she had come to love. She was already thinking about changing around her balcony at her place to be a little cozier. Maybe adding some potted plants and some cushioned chairs.

After showering and dressing, she packed up all of her things and they set out. She was slightly surprised when they stepped outside, and a slick black car was waiting for them.

After putting her suitcase in the truck and their backpacks in the back seat, Justin climbed in behind the wheel.

"Ready?" he asked as he pulled away from the hotel.

"As ready as I'll ever be," she replied. She waited until they were off the busy streets and then said, "So, tell me more about your family's place."

"Well, there's not much more to tell. It's been in the family for... generations. I don't remember how many.

Dante's father, Damiano, turned it over to Dante and Airlea when they married. Damiano and Kathleen, Dante's mother, live in a guest house they built on the property so they can be close to the grandkids. They spend a few months each year in the States, where Katie lives with her family in Seattle."

"Okay," she said. "I've heard this bit. Tell me about the olives." She smiled. "What kind? How many? And, more important, how soon can I try them?"

He laughed and then answered all the questions she had. She'd had a thing for olives for as long as she could remember. They were her salty sin. Or so her father called them.

She knew she was chatting about everything other than Madison on the long drive. They stopped in a small town and had sandwiches and soup for lunch. The conversation turned to Robin and Blake.

She'd talked to her sister earlier that morning, and she filled him in on everything her sister had gone through with the kidnapping and how she was settling in at Blake's place in Georgia. From the sounds of it, her sister was completely over the kidnapping and totally in love with Blake.

Claire was happy for Robin and couldn't wait to get back to the States. Robin had assured her that they would plan a trip to Colorado to visit.

As far as Claire could tell, Robin planned on moving to Georgia to be with Blake. It wasn't as if her sister was at her home in California a lot. In the past few years, Claire had only visited Robin's apartment in San Diego a handful of times since Robin usually spent eleven months out of the year filming on location.

Claire didn't envy her sister. Sure, she'd love to travel a little more than she had in the past, but Castle Rock was home and she loved being there. Loved everything about the town.

After they had been traveling for another hour, her phone rang. Smiling, she answered her sister's call.

"Don't freak out," Robin said when she answered.

"Okay," Claire said slowly. "Why would I be freaking out?"

"You haven't..." Robin sighed. "Okay, good. You haven't seen the news."

"No." Claire glanced over at Justin. "We're in a car heading to Justin's family's olive grove. Why? What?"

"First off, Blake did not get shot outside his office. Second—"

"Whoa." Claire held up her hands. "Wait, what?"

Robin sighed. "He did not get shot on live television. Second, we finally caught the bitch."

"Okay," she said slowly. "Why don't you start at the beginning?"

As she listened to her sister explain everything that she and Blake had gone through in the past forty-eight hours, they entered another large city. Since she'd been listening to her sister's crazy story, she didn't know where they were.

That was until she saw a sign for the Basilica of Santa Maria Novella. Her sister's story was wrapping up as Justin parked in front of a tall yellow building.

"We're in Florence," she answered her sister's question. "We just got here. I'm not sure what our plans are yet..."

"We'll stay the night here." Justin motioned to the hotel, so Claire relayed the details to her sister before hanging up with her.

"I figured you'd want a day or two here," Justin said with a smile. "It was supposed to be a surprise." He shrugged. "Surprise," he said weakly, causing her to laugh.

"Let's go check in and then you can tell me all about what's happened. From the sound of it, it's a lot."

She nodded quickly. "I was pretty bummed out that I wasn't going to be able to see Florence," she admitted as they gathered their things and stepped into the hotel. "I suppose this one is owned by your cousin too?"

"No, a friend of his," Justin said. "I'm assured that he's arranged everything again." He smiled. "I can't remember any time we've come back to Italy that our trips weren't planned out in this fashion."

"Like I said, it must be nice to have family," she said as they stepped up to the counter.

Their room was nice. Not as nice as the last one, but still nicer than the one she'd booked online. It was a massive room with the bedroom and sitting room connected via a large archway. The balcony doors led out to small balcony that overlooked the Ponte Vecchio bridge over the Arno River.

"Much nicer than what I'd booked," she said, leaning into the sunlight and smelling the warm air as she listened to the sounds of the city. She turned to see Justin tucking the mask into the safe inside the room. "Think it will be safe there?" she asked.

He nodded and then tucked something into his back pocket. "I've removed the cipher. It'll be on me at all times from here on out."

She frowned as she walked towards him. "Do you think that's wise? They've already killed once for it."

"Twice," he said with a heavy sigh. "Gina messaged me while you were on the phone with your sister that Raita didn't make it."

"Oh no." Claire frowned as she walked into his arms. "Now what?" she asked into his chest.

He wrapped his arms around her tighter. "Now we go out and try to forget about everything and enjoy ourselves while we explore Florence." He leaned down and brushed his lips across hers, and she melted into his embrace. With him by her side, she could easily forget everything bad in life and only focus on the good. Being with him.

CHAPTER SIXTEEN

Justin hadn't really explored Florence before. During all of his travels over the years to Italy, his time was usually spent with family, not visiting all of the tourist traps.

Their first stop was to the museums, where they strolled around and enjoyed seeing everything from the famous statue of David to the Birth of Venus by Sandro Botticelli.

Shortly after sunset, they found a restaurant and sat overlooking the Baptistery of St. John church. He'd forgotten how massive the place was. Each time he saw the sandstone and marble building again, he was in awe of its sheer size.

When Claire ordered a burger, he chuckled. "Tired of eating authentic food already?" he asked.

"No, just… in the mood for a burger." She shrugged. "What about you?" She motioned to him. "You ordered a burger too."

He laughed. "It sounded good."

"Burgers and beers." She laughed. "We're such tourists."

"Hey, it's nice to play one every now and then," he joked.

"So," she said after it grew quiet, "are we going to talk about it?"

"What? The Madison thing?" he asked. "I don't know what else there is that we can say about it."

"No." She smiled. "About us."

"Now that I'd be happy to talk about. What do you want to know?" He leaned forward, eagerly.

She sipped her beer, watching him. "So, I've really enjoyed sleeping in the same bed as you."

His heart did a little jump, and his smile grew. "Okay."

"I was thinking..." She leaned her elbows on the table and rested her chin in her hands. "Your place or mine?"

"Mine," he said quickly. "I've got a three-bedroom house outside of town while you are paying too much for your studio apartment."

She nodded slowly. "Okay, I can make an exception for you and move outside of town again."

He chuckled. "It's a five-minute drive into town."

"Yeah, but you know how much I like driving." She rolled her eyes.

"That's because your car is shit," he joked. "I wouldn't want to drive it either."

"That's a true story. But for now, it's what I have. Not all of us can afford a new Jeep."

He smiled. "Tip money." He looked at her mischievously. "Maybe you should work part-time waiting tables?"

She laughed. "I did that for a summer, remember? I ended up owing your dad more for broken dishes than I earned in tips."

He laughed, remembering how many times she'd

dropped full platers of food or drinks. "Okay, so not waiting tables."

"No." She smiled. "I'm seriously thinking about renting the place across from you like you suggested."

"It's a good idea. It's the right size for something like what you had planned. Plus, its right in the heart of town. You'd have a lot of foot traffic."

"Do you know who owns it?"

He laughed. "My dad does." He shook his head. "Correction, my mother does. She purchased it a couple of years back hoping to show my dad up when they had an argument about her wasting her money on redecorating. She purchased the building and, within a year, made enough to redecorate their entire house." He laughed as he remembered how proud his father was of his mother.

"Seriously? Your mother owns the building?" Claire asked. When he nodded, she shook her head. "How much is she asking for rent?"

"You'll have to bring that up with her. I have no clue."

Claire pulled out her phone and, after frowning at it, glanced up as if she was thinking.

"It's about noon there," he added with a smile.

Smiling, Claire sent a text to his mother. "There, done." She set her phone down but kept glancing at it while they ate. By the time their dessert and coffees were served, his mother had responded.

"She only wants a thousand a month for the place." Claire's eyes narrowed. "You told her I was going to ask after the place, didn't you?"

He shrugged. "Actually, she told me to mention to you that the place was empty the next time I saw you."

"Something tells me your parents planned this whole thing," she said after a minute.

"What whole thing?"

"This." She waved between them. "You in Venice at the same time I was."

He laughed. "Right. They planned my cousin's wedding." He stopped laughing when he remembered that his mother had encouraged Claire to go to Venice and, more important, had hinted about when to go.

"See." She pointed at him. "Now you believe the conspiracy theory too."

He laughed as he sipped his coffee. "If my parents managed to pull that plan off, then they are seriously super masterminds."

When they returned to their room, they spent a few moments deciding which sights they would visit the following day. When he'd been a kid, his parents had taken him and his sister to a friend's winery just outside of town. He thought it would be fun if they rented scooters for the day and enjoyed some of the countryside that surrounded the city. He was surprised when Claire was excited about the idea. He booked the scooters for the following morning.

That night when he was lying in bed with Claire happily sleeping half on his chest, her hair in his face and her legs tangled in his, his mind refused to shut down. Untangling himself from her, he pulled out his cell phone and scrolled through Madison's latest social media posts.

After last night, she hadn't posted anything on any platforms. He did a little more digging into her family.

Harrison Hayes was the third generation of his family to run Hayes Industries, a large weapons manufacturing company that supplied more than one nation with guns and ammo. Madison's father was seventy years old but still very hands-on with the company. He traveled a lot, and most of the pictures of the man were from board meetings. Madison's mother, Loralee Lynn, was always photographed at social events, most of which were high-dollar charity events.

It appeared that the seventy-year-old and his forty-something wife were rarely photographed together. Neither of them had any pictures with their daughter in the past few years. The last public photo of the family that Madison appeared in was during her early teens.

After almost an hour of scouring through the internet, he pulled Claire into his arms and clocked out.

When he woke, Claire was already in the shower. He chuckled at her singing a very off-tune version of "Stand by Me." He climbed out of bed and stepped into the shower just as she finished singing.

"You're in the wrong business," he said, pulling her into his arms. "You should be on the stage with your sister."

Claire laughed. "I've been booed off the karaoke stage enough times to know I should stick to singing in the shower." She leaned up and kissed him. "Now, *you* have some pipes on you. The last time you sang 'The Dance,' you had half the bar swooning at your feet. And not just the female half," she joked.

He chuckled. "Excited for today?"

"I've always wanted to drive a motorcycle," she said, rinsing her hair. He laughed and she frowned. "What?"

"A scooter is not a motorcycle," he clarified.

"Sure, it is." She tilted her head at him.

"No, it's not. They are as different as..." He thought about it. "As a kite and a fighter jet. One is a well-oiled sexy machine while the other is just fun for the family."

She laughed. "Why don't you have a motorcycle then?"

"Who says I don't?" he countered, and her eyebrows arched. "Okay, I don't, but I've always wanted one."

"Well, today we can pretend the scooters are Harleys."

He laughed again. "Let's head down and eat some breakfast, then go grab the scooters and hit the open road."

Madison was going to enjoy getting her revenge.

How dare Justin and Claire treat her the way they had? It was to their benefit to play along with the game. After all, up until now, she'd made it very clear to Rubio that the young couple shouldn't be harmed.

But after last night, the gloves were off. Now it was her time to plot her revenge while figuring out how to get her hands on the list.

This was no longer just about making the drop for Carmine.

She watched the couple climb on their scooters and smiled. How easy could they make it for her? She thought about revving the engine of her custom Aston Martin Vulcan, but then realized there were too many witnesses around. Instead, she watched as Justin explained to Claire how to drive a scooter, something Madison wouldn't be caught dead doing.

It took almost fifteen minutes before they headed very slowly down the busy street. By the time they turned on the main road that headed out of town, they were going a little over thirty miles per hour.

At this pace, it was going to take them all day just to get out of the city. She grew more impatient and had to hold herself back from blasting past them. What she needed was a backup plan.

Yanking the wheel, she turned around and gunned it, blasting past all the stupid tourists until she hit the open road. She had plenty of time to catch up with the couple.

After all, she knew exactly where they were heading, thanks to all of the Cardone's connections. The road they were on now would lead them to a winery that was owned by a family friend, or so Dante's social media boasted. There was more than one picture of the man and his family dining at the restaurant on site or strolling through the fields of grapes.

The way they'd been heading, it was no doubt they were on their way to Dante and Airlea's place just outside of Rome.

She remembered Claire talking about wanting to visit Florence and had figured right that the couple would take a break during the drive.

Her only problem was that time was running out. She had one week left to get the list back to New York or the game was over.

CHAPTER SEVENTEEN

Claire laughed into the wind as she gunned the gas. How could she have known that driving a scooter would be so much fun?

"Having fun?" Justin yelled over the engines.

"Yes!" She laughed some more. The countryside they were passing was beyond beautiful. The rolling paved roads were like a rollercoaster weaving through the hills. Here, the homes were few and far between.

She wanted to take some more time to explore the architecture styles but didn't want to take her eyes off the road for too long. It had taken her almost a full hour of driving the scooter before she'd relaxed enough to go the speed limit.

"We're going to be taking a right up here," Justin said, motioning to a smaller gravel road.

She slowed way down. She was nervous enough about driving on the smooth surface and now there would be potholes and large rocks to avoid.

When they pulled into the parking lot and parked, she stood there, holding the scooter while he put his kickstand down. He moved over to her as she turned off her scooter and helped her put her kickstand down.

She removed her helmet and hugged him. "That was so much fun."

He laughed. "That's good to know because it would have been a long ride back if you hadn't enjoyed the trip up here."

"This place is amazing," she said as they started walking up the gravel pathway towards the main building.

Rows and rows of grapevines spread out over the green hills below the stone and stucco buildings of the winery. The first building was a tasting room with a small store attached. A stone courtyard sat between it and the restaurant, above which vines of grapes hung. Large clusters of grapes dangled overhead for anyone to easily reach up and sample. Since the buildings sat high above the fields beyond, the views were spectacular any way you looked out over the fields.

Behind them was a tall stone staircase leading up to an older stone building that loomed over the first two.

"Hungry?" Justin asked her as they stepped into the courtyard.

"Yes," she replied. It had taken them almost two hours to drive there. She figured it would have been a half hour drive in a car.

They decided to sit outside at a table in the courtyard area. Justin ordered them a sampling of available wines. They tried several different varieties and were told all about them. They picked their favorite and ordered a bottle. Breadsticks were delivered to their table while they waited for their meals.

"Have you been here before?" she asked him after snapping a couple pictures.

"Once. We held one of my cousin's birthdays here a few years back." He looked out over the view. "It's even more beautiful than I remember it."

"It reminds me of the painting that is hanging up in your place," she said. He tilted his head in question. "Well, it used to be, before you guys redecorated a few years back. The old gold-framed painting that used to hang on the back wall." She rested her elbows on the table and cupped her chin as she sipped the wine. "That painting is the reason I've dreamed of coming to Italy my entire life."

"Really?" He chuckled. "It's hanging up at my parents' place. My great-great uncle painted it. He was somewhat of a legend in the family. A few of his paintings are hanging in a museum somewhere."

"That's exciting." She watched him, enjoying that he looked so relaxed. His hair was matted down from the helmet, but he was just as sexy as he'd ever been.

She probably looked like a wreck and, after realizing it, excused herself to the bathroom to freshen up.

When she returned, Justin was hugging a very pregnant woman while a man with a young boy stood by, smiling. Claire instantly recognized Justin's cousins. She'd met the couple a few years back when they'd visited Colorado for a winter vacation.

She hadn't met their son or, for that matter, known that she was pregnant again.

"There she is." Justin took Claire's hand when she stopped next to him. "Claire, you remember my cousin, Katie, her husband, Jason. Their son, Ash," Justin reached down and gave the little boy of around seven years old a high five.

"Justin," the boy cheered happily.

"And this is..." He motioned to Katie's stomach.

Katie laughed. "A surprise." She rolled her eyes as she ran her hands over her belly.

"Nice to see you again," Claire said.

"You as well. Dante told us you were in Italy," Jason said.

"He didn't mention you were," Justin countered as he motioned to the empty chairs. After everyone settled in, Katie answered.

"We just arrived today. We missed the wedding, but then again, I'm not that close to Isabella," Katie explained. "Still, we figured it would be a great time to visit, before we're stuck at home changing diapers. We just wanted to enjoy the day and decided to come have lunch here. It's fate we are here at the same time."

"We'll be heading down to the family's place tomorrow," Justin said.

"We heard. It'll be nice to have the family together again," Jason said. He helped Ash sit straight in the chair.

"So, Claire, Airlea told me that this is your dream trip?" Katie asked.

While Claire started explaining to Katie how long she'd waited for this trip, Justin and Jason talked quietly. Ash colored in a notebook Jason produced for him.

Shortly after their food was delivered, an extremely thin older woman came out to their table and cheerfully greeted Justin, Katie, and Jason.

"Claire, this is Donna Paxe Cattaneo. Her family owns Cattaneo winery," Justin explained.

"Nice to meet you." Claire shook the woman's hand. "You have a beautiful place and excellent wine. I plan on ordering a case, although I'm not sure how I'm going to get it back since we rented scooters."

The older woman chuckled. "We can ship." She patted

Claire's shoulder. "I just had to come say hello when Mirabel mentioned you were here." She motioned towards their server.

"You know us. If we're within fifty miles of the winery, we're going to make the stop," Jason said with a smile.

"I have a special dessert today, when you're finished with your meal, which I'll let you get back to," Donna Paxe said with a smile. "Enjoy."

"Can you believe that woman still works in the kitchen each and every day?" Katie said with a shake of her head. "It makes me exhausted just thinking about it."

Jason chuckled. "Now adays you get exhausted just walking into the kitchen." He wrapped his arm around his wife's shoulders.

"What's even more impressive is that she's pushing one hundred," Justin added. He looked at his cousin. "Not that creating a whole other person isn't impressive, but..." He shrugged.

"I asked her once what kept her going. She claimed the key to good health and long life was a glass of good wine for breakfast, chocolate, and the love of family," Katie said, holding onto her husband's hand. "I plan on living just like Donna Paxe for the rest of my life."

Claire looked over at Justin and realized the one thing she'd been missing the most in life was sitting directly across from her and how important Justin had been to her.

After lunch, they parted from Katie and Jason and strolled through the gift shop. Claire purchased a case of wine and had it shipped home, then she bought a few smaller trinkets, such as a T-shirt and a ball cap she really liked that read "Wine is the answer" along with the winery's logo.

They climbed back on the scooters with her purchases safely locked in the bin on the back.

"We'll take a different path back," Justin said as they made their way down the bumpy road. "If I can find them, there are some windmills I think you'd like to see."

"Lead the way," she said as they reached the smooth surface of the main road.

Instead of turning right, they headed left, farther away from Florence. She lost herself in thought as they twisted through the green hills with the warm air hitting her face.

They turned a corner and Justin pulled to the side of the road. She stopped next to him and followed his gaze.

There, in the distance, stood four perfectly uniform white windmills in the middle of a beautiful green field.

"It's perfect," Claire said as she pulled out her phone and snapped a few pictures.

"I thought you'd like it. They're called quattro sorelle, four sisters. They were built almost four hundred years ago and still supply water to the town."

"I love them. Thank you." She smiled and then snapped a picture of Justin as he stood there, holding his scooter with the windmills behind him.

Justin was laughing when they both heard the high-pitched squeal of the car wheels. Claire didn't even have a moment to react or brace before the scooter was jerked out from under her.

Her arms and legs seemed to all go in different directions as she flew through the air. She heard Justin scream, and, in that instant, she no longer cared about the coming pain. Instead, she desperately worried about him. Had he been hit too?

She didn't have any time to brace, and the moment she hit the ground, her body rolled in the grass. Her clothes tore and one of her shoes flew off. She would never forget the sound that the helmet made when it hit a few rocks on the ground.

Everything faded to black before her body came to a stop at the bottom of a small hill.

"It's done. Do what you need to." Madison smiled as she hung up the phone and punched the gas, sending the Aston Martin speeding through the side roads.

God, she felt good. The high that came with each kill made her float higher than any drug she'd tried in her teens.

Rubio would take care of the rest. He'd already gotten the mask from the hotel and was on his way to meet her. When he'd called and told her he had it, she'd almost backed out of taking care of Justin and Claire. But then she'd remembered the embarrassment they'd caused her the other night and craved revenge. Besides, she was having too much fun.

Sure, the Aston Martin would have to go into the shop, but she wouldn't be needing it for a few months anyway. Besides, she was thinking of having the paint updated. Maybe a panther style paint job?

Something that screamed dangerous.

CHAPTER EIGHTEEN

J ustin woke with a start. Pain shot through his elbow and hip. He was twisted at an odd angle and lying in what appeared to be grass, looking up at the sky.

His first thought was of Claire. Then he remembered seeing her fly through the air after the sports car had hit her scooter.

"Claire!" He tried to cry out for her, but her name came out as a squeak instead.

Taking a moment to assess himself, he realized that, although everything hurt, nothing appeared broken. He was bleeding from a couple scrapes. He rolled onto his hands and knees, removed his helmet, and started looking for Claire.

He found her at the bottom of the hill. Her helmet was still in place and, much like he'd been, she was lying flat on her back. Her eyes were closed but she had a strong pulse.

"Claire?" He brushed his fingers across her face. He didn't want to remove the helmet or move her just yet.

Relief washed over him when her eyelids fluttered open.

"Justin?" she said softly. "I had a strange dream."

"Don't move baby. I've got you. Tell me where it hurts." He ran his hands over her arms and legs.

She winced when he touched her left wrist. "Just... everywhere. What happened?" she asked as he helped her sit up slowly.

"A car. It appeared to be aiming for us." He thought back to what he could remember about the Aston Martin. He'd seen Madison behind the wheel. "It was Madison," he said as Claire bent down and touched her leg. She gasped and looked up at him. Before saying anything else, she slowly removed her helmet.

He noticed that her knuckles were bloody and looked down at his own bloody hands.

"Hell, we're a mess, but it appears we're okay," he said with relief after he helped her stand up. She was a little wobbly, but whole. Healthy. Alive. They both were. He pulled her into his arms and held onto her. "I don't know what I would have done if..." He felt a knot in his throat and pulled back to run his eyes over her once more. She had a scrape on her chin, dried blood on her cheek. "I love you. It's probably a shitty time, but..."

She rushed up on her toes and kissed him until he relaxed and held onto her.

"I love you too," she said with a smile. "I have for a very long time."

"Same." He chuckled and took her hand in his.

"The scooters are destroyed," she said after a moment.

He glanced over and, sure enough, both machines lay in ruin, parts strewn all over the green grass and hillside.

"It appears as if they took the brunt of the force. Thankfully."

"How will we get back?" she asked him.

He looked around. "Help me find my phone. I'll call Katie. And I'll have to get my family involved. She's crossed the line this time," he said. "We're past the point of trying to deal with this ourselves."

"What about the cops? We rented the scooters. They'll want to know what happened."

When they found his phone, the screen was cracked but it still worked. He called Katie first, then the police.

Katie and Jason got there almost five minutes before the police showed up.

Claire was sitting in their rental car while he and Jason talked along the road. He filled him in on everything that had happened and even showed him the cipher. Before the police arrived, he asked him not to mention the cipher to the police. Instead, they would just explain what type of car had hit them and tell them they recognized the driver, explaining that they knew Madison personally but were unclear why she would wish them harm.

"Until we know more about it, let's keep the cipher quiet," he said, and Jason agreed.

"Later, remind me to tell you about Katie's and my first trip through Greece and Italy," Jason said with a smile.

"When Aunt Florentina tried to have the both of you killed?" he asked. Jason nodded.

"Yeah, but if it wasn't for that crazy trip, we would have remained just friends." Jason glanced over at him, smiling. "Like the two of you."

Justin looked across the way at Claire and frowned. He'd like to think that he would have eventually made a move. At some point he would have grown the balls to ask her out. To lean over and kiss her just once.

But the truth was, if they hadn't been halfway across the world in Venice, he probably wouldn't have made a move.

"Still, I think we could do without some sociopath trying to kill us." He walked over as the police arrived.

"What do we do now?" Claire asked when they were heading back towards their hotel, crammed in Jason and Katie's rental. Ash was fast asleep in his car seat, and everyone was talking quietly.

"Now?" Justin thought about it. "I think we should cut our time in Florence short and head to the family's place with Katie and Jason tonight."

They were in over their heads in all this. He needed time to think but he was in too much pain. Everything hurt. His muscles were so tense, he doubted he could sit or stand without grunting at this point.

When they got to their hotel, Jason went up with them to gather their things while Katie and Ash waited in the parked car.

The moment they stepped into their room; they both knew something was wrong. The safe sat wide open and, once again, their things were thrown around the room.

"I'm getting seriously tired of having to clean up after that woman," Claire said with a groan.

"Well, she took the mask," Justin said, shutting the safe.

"Why? Didn't she notice the cipher was gone?" Claire asked.

Justin smiled and held in a chuckle. "No, because I put a fake one in its place."

Claire's eyes widened. "You did?" She started laughing and immediately winced. "Oh my god. That is so... brilliant," she said with a sigh. "So, what? She now thinks that she killed us and has the cipher."

"I'm hoping it will buy us a few days to talk to my uncle and see if he has some connections to ensure you're cleared of Gabriele Lombardi's death."

"Who?" Jason asked.

He'd forgotten his cousin's husband was there and sighed. He'd told him the basics but hadn't mentioned Gabriele Lombardi's or Raita's deaths.

While they packed up their things, he filled Jason in on all the other details.

"What about calling the police about the break-in?" Claire asked him when they were leaving.

"I'm too tired," he said. "Besides, we know the only thing they got away with was the mask. Nothing in the room was damaged this time so the hotel won't be concerned."

"Right."

It wasn't until they walked through the lobby to check out that he realized people were staring at them. Glancing down, he realized they should have at least showered and changed out of their bloody and torn clothes.

"I guess we should have showered," Claire said as they started driving away.

"Three hours and we'll be at my cousin's place. Can you hang on until then?" he asked. When she nodded, he reached over and took her hand. "We should have gone to the hospital—"

"I'm fine," she broke in. "Just cuts and bruises. You?"

"Same. Along with sore muscles."

"Yeah." She relaxed back. "Will you be okay driving?"

"Yeah," he answered. He wanted some time to think, and the drive would be perfect. He followed Jason and Katie onto the main highway. They'd agreed to stick close to one another on the drive. Just to be safe.

He was pretty sure that Madison believed she'd killed them and that she was now in possession of the cipher. Even though he'd written the characters on a piece of blank paper from the hotel room, he'd done his best to make it appear old like the other one.

He had even torn it like the real one was. As for the cipher, he'd used all of the characters that had been on the original message, but he'd jumbled them up and left out a few as well.

When he glanced over, Claire was fast asleep, and he knew she was thankful for having the time to recover. He could use a long hot shower and a soft bed himself.

How long would they have before Madison would figure things out? Did she even know what the cipher said? He doubted that she'd get word that they were still alive. After all, the police report wouldn't be advertised or reported about in any of the local papers.

His mind ran through everything he'd learned in the past week, everything that had happened to them. Everything pointed to Madison Hayes being a sociopath. Someone who didn't care about anyone else or even herself.

He'd seen her eyes as she'd aimed her very expensive car towards them. There had been excitement there. The thrill of killing. He wondered if she'd been the one to pull the trigger with Gabriele and Raita.

No, she'd been having dinner with them at the wedding. And there was the large man that had attacked them and stolen Claire's luggage.

She was definitely working with someone. After all, while she'd been plowing them down with her car, someone else had been breaking into their hotel room, just like the other times.

For the first hour or so on the road, he ran everything over in his mind. Then his mind wandered to him and Claire, to their future together and how he was going to try and convince her to marry him.

Hell, it had been her idea to move in together. He smiled at that and for the first time since being thrown from the scooter, he relaxed. They'd told one another that they loved each other. It hadn't been under the best circumstances, but still, he could fix that. The family's olive grove was one of the most romantic places he could think of in Italy.

He remembered the lake on the family's property and thought about having a picnic by the water. Of sitting in the shade of one of the olive trees and telling Claire just how he felt.

That thought helped him through the next hour and half of driving. When they turned off the main road, Claire woke up. She blinked a few times, stretched, and asked how close they were.

"The gate is just ahead," he said, motioning. "How are you feeling?"

"Sore." She leaned closer to get a good view ahead.

Two large iron gates that read Cardone Olive Grove blocked the private lane.

They stopped behind Jason and Katie and waited as they punched in the code to unlock the gates.

He knew the codes himself, but since the gate allowed them to pass through as well, he followed them up the road and over the hillside until they came to the top, where the main house sat.

The large mansion had been handed down for over six generations now. There were acres and acres of olive tree groves and vineyards surrounding the half-stone, half-stucco building with its classic, red-tiled roof. It was surrounded by rolling hills, olive trees, and rows and rows of grapevines. The view was spectacular from every window in the place.

There was a large swimming pool with a pool house

behind the main building. Justin knew that the newer building that housed Dante and Katie's parents sat just beyond the hillside behind the home.

There was a large stone archway with a huge balcony that ran across the front of the house and down both sides. Ornate black iron railings and huge stone pillars held up the balcony and stopped waist high on the second level. Rows of French doors lined the front of the home on both the main floor and the upper floor.

The place somehow managed to look better each time he visited. This time, there were fresh flowers in the large pots that sat along the front.

As they parked, Dante and Airlea came outside along with their girls, Camilla and Cora.

He was home. Even though he had never lived here, this place was as familiar to him as the home his parents still lived in, clear across the world from here.

This is what he wanted with Claire. A place they could call their own. Somewhere they could raise their own children and grow old together. Until now, he hadn't realized that all he'd ever wanted was her.

CHAPTER NINETEEN

There was just too much beauty to take in all at once and Claire's head was spinning. Meanwhile, every muscle in her body ached. At this point, even her teeth ached.

Still, the nap in the car had helped a little. She probably felt a great deal better than Justin did at this point.

They were showed to a guest room upstairs. She followed Justin like a zombie around the place and, after grabbing a change of clothing, she stepped into the hot shower along with him.

She stood like a statue while he gently wiped her cuts and removed the dried blood from her skin. Airlea had given them a first aid kit and, once they were both cleaned, they spent some time bandaging up the worst of their cuts.

After that, they both lay down on the bed and fell into a deep sleep.

She woke sometime after dark when she heard children's laughter somewhere in the house. It was such a foreign sound to her. It had been too long since she'd been around kids, and it took her a moment to remember where she was.

"Are you okay?" Justin's voice sounded beside her. Then he shifted and a low light filled the room.

"Yeah. You?"

"Sore but rested and starving." He shifted and pulled her into his arms. "I'm sure my cousin has dinner all ready for us."

It was then that she smelled the wonderful scent of bread and spices, and her stomach growled loudly.

"We can head down," she suggested as she melted into his chest.

"I want to hold you for just a minute," he said into her hair. "I thought I was going to lose you today," he said, making her heart jump.

"Me too," she admitted as she closed her eyes tightly, blocking out what had happened earlier.

"I'm going to make things right. Make it safe for us. The police are looking for Madison, but something tells me that even if they arrest her, she won't stay locked away for long."

"Not with how much money her family has," she agreed.

"But at least it would get out there. The story of what she did."

"We're bad guests," she said after hearing the kids laughing again.

She felt his chuckle vibrate his body. "We're not guests. We're family," he corrected.

"I'm not," she said.

He rolled over and looked down at her. "You are if you're with me." He kissed her. "And you are definitely with me."

After they freshened up, they made their way downstairs. Now she was far more awake and alert to assess the beautiful home.

The place was nothing like what she'd imagined a home that had been in the same family for five generations would look like.

It had old-world Italian charm in the stone pillars that ran on each side of the kitchen area. There was a cozy dining room with a massive family-sized dining table.

But instead of an older, outdated kitchen, there were marble countertops, new cupboards, and top-of-the-line appliances.

"Oh, you're awake," Airlea said when she spotted them standing in the archway. The woman rushed across the room and hugged her. "Are you okay?"

"I am." Claire felt her eyes sting and had to swallow her tears. She hadn't been emotional so far and didn't plan on starting now. Not with everyone filling the kitchen and watching them.

"Come on in," Katie said as she stirred the contents of a bowl. "Dinner is almost ready."

Just then the back door opened, and three kids came rushing in, followed by two small dogs and an older woman carrying a bundle of freshly cut flowers.

"Katie, dear, did you know that Cora's got another loose tooth?" the woman said. She stopped when she spotted them. "Justin," she said. She set the flowers down to rush across the room and hug him. "And this must be Claire." The woman wrapped her arms around her. "I'm Kathleen, Katie and Dante's mother."

"Yes, I've heard a lot about you," she responded. Whatever she'd expected from the stories she'd heard of Kathleen Cardone, the woman standing in front of her didn't fit her imaginings.

Kathleen had stylish shoulder-length silver hair. She wore a summer dress with flowers on it and even had one in her hair. The warm smile on her face was genuine, and her eyes twinkled with kindness. The woman was stunningly beautiful.

"Damiano is out gathering some herbs," Kathleen said, taking her hand. "Come sit down. Katie filled us all in on what the two of you have been through." She held out a chair at a smaller kitchen table that sat just inside two glass doors that looked out to the pool area. "How are you feeling?" she asked both of them as Justin sat next to her.

"Sore," they both said at the same time.

"I fell off my friend's dirt bike once in middle school. I thought that I hurt after that, but this..." Justin shrugged as his eyes landed on her. "Nothing beats getting hit by a car."

"I got bucked off a horse once," Katie said.

"Not to mention you jumped out of a moving van," Dante added

"At least I didn't get hit by it like you did," Katie joked. She walked over and wrapped her arms around her brother.

For the first time, Claire could see the resemblance between the two of them. Maybe it was because she'd finally met their mother? Then Damiano Cardone walked in the back door, a basket of herbs in his arms, and suddenly it was very obvious the two were brother and sister.

She and Justin didn't move a muscle the entire time that dinner was being prepared. The kids rushed around until Kathleen suggested they head out and jump in the pool until the food was ready. Damiano and Jason disappeared to watch them swim, while Dante and the rest finished preparing the meal.

Kathleen opened a bottle of wine from the Cattaneo winery and poured them each a glass.

When the food was ready, the kids were shuffled in, dried off, and everyone moved into the larger dining room.

Claire had, in the past, had plenty of dinners with Justin and his family. She knew that his family dinners could be loud and entertaining, but she could have never been prepared for sitting in a room full of Cardones.

There were no fewer than three conversations going at any single time. Stories were told and retold as laughter echoed in the house. Several more bottles of wine were passed around and by the time the tiramisu was served, the alcohol had eliminated most of Claire's aches and pains from the accident earlier.

"You know what the two of you need?" Airlea said, waving her wine glass in the air. "You need to go sit in the hot tub and soak away the rest of the pain. Then, in the morning"—she sipped her wine— "late morning, I'll give you both massages."

"She gives the best massages," Katie chimed in.

"I'll agree with that," Jason and Dante said at the same time, causing several people to laugh.

"I don't think we'd ever turn down a free massage," Justin said, winking at Claire. "Right, babe?"

"Right." She sighed. "A soak in the hot tub sounds good. I miss the sauna in our room back in Milan." She set her glass down, then turned to Justin. "We need one at your place back home."

He nodded. "That can be arranged." He took her hand.

"So, the two of you are living together then?" Kathleen asked.

Claire looked to Justin, who smiled at her. "We will be when we get back home."

"How wonderful. Do your parents know?" Kathleen asked.

Justin chuckled. "No, Aunt Kathleen, you know something my mother doesn't." He lifted his glass. "Feel free to gloat."

She chuckled and held up her own wine glass. "Oh, I will."

It was strange. The dinner took more than two hours, yet it felt as if it passed by in a flash. They were told to go enjoy the hot tub while everyone else cleaned up the mess. The kids were shuffled upstairs, bathed, and put to bed while she and Justin changed into their swimsuits.

When they walked back downstairs, the house was quiet.

"It's past nine," Justin said. "The family will be asleep soon enough. Life on a ranch like this starts very early," he said as they stepped outside onto the pool deck. "The hot tub is over here." He motioned to the side of the deck. "Want a dip in the pool to cool off first?"

"Sure." She pulled off the shorts and T-shirt she'd put on over her suit, then jumped into the cool water with as big of a splash as she could.

When she surfaced, Justin followed, making sure to splash her with the water. His hands wrapped around her waist, and she had a moment to hold her breath before he pulled her under the water again.

When they surfaced, breathless and laughing, they wrapped themselves around each other.

"What are the chances of you building a pool at your place?" she asked.

He laughed. "For now, I think we might have to do with a hot tub."

"I'll take it." She kicked off and started floating on her back with him beside her.

"How are the aches?" he asked.

She took a moment to assess her entire body. "Minimal." She looked at the worst of her cuts on her elbow. Then she looked at his marred skin. "You?"

His arms wrapped around her again. "Much better now," he said before he kissed her.

She felt the warmth spread throughout her entire body, from her lips down to her toes.

"My god, Claire," Justin said against her skin. "Let's move over to the hot tub where its more private."

He kicked towards the edge of the pool, then surprised her by lifting her into his arms and carrying her towards the hot tub. He set her on the bench as he lifted the lid and turned on the bubbles. Then he picked her up again and set her in the water.

He climbed in behind her, pulled her into his arms again, and continued kissing her. His hands went to her hips, only this time, he nudged her swimsuit down. He set the bottoms on the edge of the hot tub and cupped her, causing a low moan to escape her lips.

"Justin," she said, his name coming out as more of a warning. Shouldn't they head upstairs? What if someone came out and saw?

"I've got you," he said next to her ear. He trailed his lips down her neck as his fingers started to move. Stars exploded behind her eyes as her body instantly reacted to his touch. She would always react as such to him. This was Justin. The man she had loved her entire life. The man she dreamed of being with for the rest of it.

CHAPTER TWENTY

In the end, they spent four nights with his family. He took Claire on walks all over their land, prepared picnics for her along the lake, and spent the entire time showing and telling her how he felt about her.

He'd never spent a more perfect time in his life. But he knew that it was only a matter of time before Madison found out that they were still alive and that he'd replaced the cipher.

Katie, Jason, and Ash left two days after they'd gotten there. What had happened with Robin and the senator was all over the news. So much so that Claire made a point to call her sister almost every day.

He noticed that she hadn't once mentioned what they'd gone through. When he asked her about it, she shrugged and casually told him that her sister had enough to worry about.

It was the same reason he hadn't told his own parents and had asked his family to let him tell his folks on his own timeline.

His aunt seemed more concerned with knowing that he

and Claire were an item before his mother did than knowing about the mess with Madison.

On that front, there wasn't a whole lot of news. The Italian police were looking for Madison, but since no one had been seriously injured during the accident, it wasn't a top priority.

Which meant Madison would probably never be charged. They talked a lot about going to the police with the cipher and what they knew about Gabriele Lombardi's death, but each time they talked about it, they decided it was just too risky. After all, Claire was the last person to see the man alive. They'd both watched enough mystery stories to know that didn't usually sit well with the police, no matter what country you were in.

"We'll be heading to Rome after we eat," he told his family over breakfast.

"I can't thank you enough for letting us stay here," Claire said.

"Any time," Damiano replied.

"This is your first of a lifetime of trips here, I'm sure of it," Kathleen said cheerfully.

"I hope so," Claire said, smiling at his family. "There is still so much I want to see. I can't believe we have less than a week left before we have to head back home."

"You're going to love Rome," Airlea said with a sigh. "We lived there until shortly after we married. When we wanted to start our family." She motioned to the girls who were watching television. "Damiano and Kathleen had their place built so we can raise them here. I miss the city sometimes, but then we take a day trip and I realize how much I don't miss it." She chuckled.

"Castle Rock is a good mix of both. It's grown so much since we were kids, but it hasn't reached a full city size. I don't think it ever will," Claire said, looking at him. "It's perfect for me."

"And me," he added quickly. "Denver is so close that if we need to get our city fix, it's just a short drive away."

"We'll have to come visit again soon," Dante said. "When my new niece or nephew is born, we'll head to the States and take a road trip with the girls."

"You're always welcome. You know that," Justin said. "All of you."

After breakfast, they packed up their things once more, said goodbye to his family, and headed out. The drive into the city wasn't as beautiful as their ride on the scooters through the country. Almost half an hour after leaving the family's place, they turned onto the main highway and the beautiful country landscape grew more crowded with buildings and traffic.

By the time they pulled up to the St. Regis hotel, the place he and Claire had decided to stay instead of at the hotel the family owned in Rome, he was hungry again.

He knew Claire would want to spend the following days hitting all the tourist spots, including museums and shopping. Today, they had planned on checking into the hotel and then exploring the shops and area immediately around their hotel. Then they would take the fifteen-minute walk over to the Fontana di Trevi before heading to the Vatican, where they had tickets for a nighttime tour.

Dante had assured them that the night tours were less crowded and allowed you more freedom to explore. Since he'd never been, he was looking forward to spending the evening strolling around and seeing the art.

He had to admit, the hotel was top notch. Even though their room just had one room and no sitting area, it was nice.

The bathroom had black marble countertops and a bathtub big enough for the two of them.

After unpacking, Claire changed into a pair of cream-colored capris and a rose-colored shirt, along with the glass heart necklace he'd purchased for her, and they headed out. The cipher was still safely tucked in his wallet.

They sat in a café overlooking the Trevi fountain and enjoyed lunch, then spent the next few hours strolling around the shops.

When he found a mask much like the one that had been stolen, he purchased it for her.

"I know it's not the same, and it's from Rome instead of Venice, but maybe it'll do." He handed it to her.

"I love it." She smiled down at the mask. "It's almost identical and doesn't have that gem that I didn't like."

"Right?" He nodded.

"This one is perfect. Thank you." She gave him a kiss. "Let's take it back to the hotel before we head over to the Vatican, so we don't have to carry around all this." She motioned to the bags filled with the other items she'd purchased.

"We can ship them?" he offered.

"Sure." She glanced around and motioned to a little store that shipped. "Everything except for..." She dug in her bag and pulled out a shirt, then held it up for him. "I bought this for you." She smiled at him. "You can wear it tonight."

It was a nice blue button-up shirt, something he would have chosen for himself.

"I like it. You have great taste." He pulled her into his arms. "Thank you."

She laughed. "What I want to do is make you something myself, but for now, I like this."

After shipping her purchases home, they went back to

the hotel where she freshened up and he changed into the new shirt. She changed out of the capris into the new skirt she'd purchased and a cream-colored top with her comfortable walking boots, which is what she called the sexy tan heeled boot that stopped just above her ankles.

"You look amazing," he said, when she stepped out of the bathroom. She did a little twirl and smiled at him. "You can't go into the Vatican looking like a total schmuck," she said, mimicking his mother's tone and voice.

He walked over and kissed her. "Agreed, but you don't sound anything like her, thankfully."

She laughed. "We can grab some dinner if we head out now," she suggested.

"Great idea." He took her hand in his. "I love you. You know that right?"

Her smile grew. "I love you too."

They had a couple of hours before they needed to check in at the north gate, so they strolled past the Trevi again, and Claire took more than three dozen pictures of them in front of the lit-up fountain. Claire decided she wanted to try a little Mediterranean place instead of looking for something local.

"We don't have enough good Mediterranean places in Colorado," Claire said after swallowing a bite of food.

"Agreed." He took another bite of the spiced meat sandwich.

After dinner, they strolled hand in hand to the Vatican and took pictures of Piazza San Pietro, or Saint Peter's Square. Then they walked around the tall walls of the city until they reached the museum gates. They stood in line and followed the rest of the crowd inside.

For the next four hours, they roamed the long hallways

of the largest museum in the country, since technically the Vatican was its own country.

His favorite paintings were the School of Athens and, of course, the Sistine Chapel ceiling by Michelangelo. Claire really enjoyed the scenery paintings and spent more time admiring them than any others.

"Just look at the dresses and outfits they wore," she said more than once.

There was far too much to look at and, before he knew it, they were walking through the gift shop looking for trinkets to prove they'd been there.

They got back to their hotel shortly before midnight and had just fallen into bed when Claire's phone rang.

He rolled over and listened to her talk quietly with her sister for a while. She told Robin where they were staying, what their plans were, and when they'd be home. She even mentioned that she'd be moving in with him when they returned. He smiled and pulled her into his arms.

He fell asleep listening to her soft voice and, when he woke, he pulled her into his arms as she woke with a yawn.

"How's Robin?" he asked into her hair.

"Good. She's officially engaged to Blake," Claire said with a sigh. "They've even made an announcement."

"She is?" He leaned back and looked at Claire's face. She appeared happy about it. "Haven't they only known one another for..."

"About a month." Claire chuckled. "Yeah, but Robin swears he's the one. I'm happy for them. I can't wait to meet the guy."

"Me too," he said in a deep voice.

Claire chuckled. "You sound like a brother trying to protect his sister."

He thought about it for a moment, then nodded. "Robin

is kind of like a sister. I'd be just as skeptical of anyone Nicky brought home."

Claire's eyebrows arched. "You've always thought of Robin like a sister. Does that mean—"

He stopped her by kissing her. "I have never once thought of you like a sister," he said smoothly.

Her smile was back. "What are we doing today?"

"I think I'm all museum-ed out," he admitted.

She nodded. "You could spend a lifetime in the Vatican and not see it all. Okay, shopping?" she asked, squishing up her nose, a move he knew meant she wasn't too into the idea.

"How about we put on our walking shoes, head over to the Colosseum for a tour, and then see what other sights we stumble upon today?" he suggested.

"That sounds like a perfect plan. What do you say we shower, get dressed, and try to find someplace nice to have breakfast?"

"Sounds like a plan." He rolled over, pinning her under him, and started trailing kisses over her flawless skin. "After."

CHAPTER TWENTY-ONE

W alking around the Colosseum was like stepping back in time. Claire could just imagine crowds of people shuffling into the stands to watch the gore and mayhem.

None of that interested her, but then again, she didn't care too much for sports either. Still, the history of the place was enough to spark her interest. After the hour-long tour, they strolled around the other historical sights surrounding the massive structure.

After the tour, they spent the rest of the day hitting all the historical sites. The Pantheon, Basilica Papale di Santa Maria Maggiore, and more gothic churches than she could remember the names of.

They ate dinner in their room and watched television since they were both too tired to dress and go out.

The following morning, she woke before Justin and decided to get some fresh air. She slipped out on their balcony and started going through all of the photos.

She'd taken so many pictures that she had to back everything up online and, while she was at it, she happily posted a few pictures to her social media. Pictures of her and Justin in front of the Colosseum, at the Vatican, and even a few at his family's olive grove. Them having a picnic by the water's edge and some of them at the winery before the accident.

When her friends started commenting on her and Justin's relationship, she replied to a few comments. So many of them were happy and said that it was about time, while others seemed slightly shocked that they were together.

Justin had just stepped out on the balcony when a message came through that chilled her and made her realize the mistake she'd just made.

"What?" Justin said, rushing over to her side.

"I... messed up." She closed her eyes and handed him her phone. "I didn't think. I... just wanted to share the amazing trip with everyone."

She waited as he scrolled through the responses from the image of them yesterday at the Colosseum. Then he got to Madison's comment and froze.

"It's okay," he said as he read. "We couldn't hide from her forever." He glanced up.

"She's crazy. Who tries to kill two people then messages them on social media like we're old friends?" She took her phone from him and looked down at the words. From an outsider's perspective, there was nothing amiss about Madison's message: "Looks like you two are having fun in Rome. I hope the rest of your trip goes as smoothly. Safe travels. - M"

Justin disappeared inside and quickly came back with his computer. After a moment, he sighed. "There's nothing in your pictures or posts that would lead her to where we're staying. Or what our plans are for the next four days until we head home." He took her hand in his. "Do you really want to be looking over our shoulder for the rest of our lives?"

She shook her head. "I... hadn't thought." She closed her eyes. "I guess I just wasn't thinking. I'm sorry."

He smiled. "About?" She waved her hands towards his computer. "Claire, we're not going to stop our lives. We'll figure this out. I guess the first move would be to meet with Madison in some very public place and confront her."

"What about the cipher?" she asked, concerned.

He pulled it out of his wallet and looked down at it. "For all we know, she still believes she has the real one." He held it up and then stilled. "There's more here." He showed her.

"It's..." She squinted, then gasped. "Justin, do you know what this is?" She took the thin paper from him.

"It's an old piece of paper," he said, looking closer.

"This is more than just a cipher on an old piece of paper. There's code here." She held it up towards the sun, thinking. Then she gasped again. "The gem." She jumped up and rushed into the room to search through her clothes. "I put it in a pocket..." she said. She searched her jeans and her khakis, and then tried her shorts. She smiled when her fingers brushed the gem. "Here it is."

"What's that got to do with the cipher?" he asked.

"CDS," she said remembering Robin telling her about it. "Crystal data storage." She held the clear crystal up, then on a whim, walked over to her purse, pulled out her compact, and slid the crystal across the surface. When her mirror broke, she turned to Justin. "It's a diamond. One that, if I'm right, holds the data that unlocks with this code." She held up the paper. "It's not a cipher, it's a key."

"How would someone go about reading the data off this?" he asked, taking the diamond from her fingers and holding it up in the light, as if he could see the information with his own eyes.

"You'd need a reader." She tried to remember what Robin had told her. "Well, at least that's how it worked in Robin's movie, *Magnanimous*, where she played Kim Lost, superhero." Claire smiled.

"Right." He snapped his fingers. "Robin, aka, Kim Lost, discovered the secret plans to the queen's underground bunker in the diamond tiara."

She smiled. "God, I loved that movie."

"Yeah." Justin nodded. "I normally don't go for super-hero movies, but that one kicked butt. Okay, so what we have here is a lot of data someone wanted to smuggle. But Madison?" He shrugged. "What are they? Plans to her father's weapons that she's selling to the competition?"

"Could be." Claire took the gem and the paper and tucked them both in her jean pockets. "What we need is help." She turned to him. "Know anyone who is good at this sort of stuff?"

He thought about it. "I have a second uncle of sorts." He shrugged. "Katie's half-brother's wife's brother." He chuckled when she shook her head. "Yeah, I mentioned my family was complicated. Anyway, I can leave him a message?"

"Who is he? What does he do?" she asked.

"His name is Ethan Knight. He does—"

She held up her hand. "Hold on. You're related to Ethan Knight?" she asked, feeling her head spin.

"Yeah, why?" he asked, frowning.

"Ethan's the one who saved my sister and Blake. He's married to Blake's sister Ann."

"No freaking way." Justin shook his head. "Small world. Okay, so let's—"

Just then their hotel door flew open with such force, both of them were knocked on their backs. Smoke filled the room so quickly that she lost track of where she was. She couldn't even see Justin.

Fumbling around, she realized her cell phone was still in her pocket. Pulling it out, she punched redial.

"Morning," her sister answered happily.

"Robin!" Claire screamed into the phone since her ears were ringing so loud. "Help us!" she cried out just as strong arms grabbed her. She was yanked back and pulled along the floor.

She kicked out, connecting with something solid and heard a grunt as she tried to get away.

"Claire!" Justin's voice was coming from somewhere to her left.

"Justin," she cried out, only to have the hands grab at her again, this time around her waist. She was hoisted up and thrown over a man's shoulders as she continued to fight, kicking out and even scratching and biting.

The man stepped out into the hallway, and Claire could hear the fire alarms blaring throughout the hotel over her screams for help. The man took a few steps down the hallway when a body slammed into them, knocking them down. Claire landed on her shoulder and rolled to her back. Her neck hurt, and she was pretty sure she'd sprained her wrist.

Then more hands were reaching for her, and she blindly fought out.

"Claire, it's me. Get up and run," Justin said loudly.

She didn't need any further encouragement. He pulled her to her feet, and they ran together down the hallway, hand in hand. They made it to the stairs before they heard the first shot.

People screamed and ran for cover while smoke continued to fill the hallway.

"He's set the whole damn hotel on fire," Justin said, pushing his way down the stairs.

"He's shooting at us," she cried out as they rushed down the stairs with the other guests.

"I know," Justin said, glancing back.

Claire had been so preoccupied trying to get away that she hadn't even looked at the man. When they made it to the next floor, however, she glanced back and saw a tall man in a bomber jacket and dark pants, with a thin mustache.

When she locked eyes with him, he pointed his gun directly at her and smiled. She waited, dreading that each heartbeat would be her last, but he tucked his gun back into his jacket and mouthed, "Soon. You can't hide from me." Then he turned around and headed up the stairs.

She let Justin pull her down the rest of the stairs. When they reached the outside, he didn't stop running.

"He's gone," she tried to tell him, but he just kept pulling her down the side streets until they ducked into a train station. They jumped on the first train they could get on.

When the doors shut them in, he nudged her into a chair and held onto her.

"Are you okay?" he asked.

"Yes, I'm okay," she said several times while they held onto one another. "Are you hurt?"

He leaned back and ran his eyes over her. "You're wrist?" he asked after he noticed she was holding it funny.

"Sprained. I don't think it's broken." She tried to move it and winced. "Okay, maybe."

He took it in his hands and gently looked it over, moving it slightly. When she winced, he nodded. "We'll need to get it looked at." Then he looked at her. "Tell me you still have the diamond and the code."

She searched her pockets and sighed when she felt them. Pulling them out, she held them up for Justin to take.

He took them, looked around the train, and tucked them in his pocket. "It's a good thing I had my wallet and phone." He took out his phone. "Which is busted yet again."

They had stopped at a phone repair shop and had the screen fixed after the first incident. Now, it was shattered again.

"I lost my phone, and my purse was back in the room. I called my sister after the explosion." She closed her eyes. "Was that a bomb?"

"No, I think it was a concussion grenade," Justin responded. "There wasn't a lot of damage other than throwing us across the room and the smoke."

She shook her head and looked out the window of the train. "How did he find us so quickly?"

Justin shook his head. "I'm not sure." He looked down at his phone. "I'm going to call Ethan." Since his screen wasn't working, he asked Siri to call Ethan.

"Ethan, it's..." Justin started, only to stop. "Yeah, she's here. We're safe." Justin's eyes landed on her. "Your sister is with Ethan," he said, holding the phone up between them.

"Robin?" Claire cried.

"Oh my god. Are you okay?" Robin asked.

"Yes, we both are. There was..." She shook her head.

"Robin, I need to talk to Ethan," Justin broke in.

"Of course," Robin said. "Ethan?"

They heard the phone being handed over.

"What's the situation?" Ethan asked.

For the next few minutes, while the train continued on

its path, stopping at each station to let people on and off, Justin explained everything to Ethan.

"Where are you now?" she overheard Ethan ask.

Justin glanced up at the train map and then said, "We're headed towards Ostia."

The line was quiet for a few moments. "I'll call you back in five. Get off at the end of the line, then head towards the beach. I'll send you directions—"

"My screen is shot," Justin said with a sigh.

"Get it fixed. Pay cash if you've got it," Ethan suggested.

"I do. Claire lost her purse and phone, but I had my wallet and phone on me."

"Good, get the phone fixed. I'll text you where to go from there," Ethan added before hanging up.

Justin tucked his phone in his pocket and then wrapped his arms around her. "We've got about an hour before the end of the line," he said. "Why don't we go to the bathroom and try to clean up a bit, so we don't draw too much attention to ourselves?" He pulled her into his arms and kissed her again.

"This is all my fault," she said as tears rolled down her dirty cheeks. "If I hadn't posted..."

He stilled in her arms. "This is not on you. But I think that's how they found us. Your post probably tagged the hotel." He sighed. "We'll find out more when I get my screen fixed. For now"—he leaned back and cupped her face in his hands— "we're safe. We're alive. This is not," he said slowly, "your fault."

Even though he said it several more times during the hour-long train ride to the coast, she knew it was. She'd been so stupid. Like those teenagers in all the movies that end up getting killed because they were dumb. Justin deserved so much better than her.

CHAPTER TWENTY-TWO

Following Ethan's direction, they got off the train at the last stop in the coastal town of Ostia. Crowds of tourists were gathered around the town square, where a market was taking place, and along the pebble-covered beaches and the boardwalk shops.

After replacing his phone's screen again, they found a café and sat in the back and had some coffee, waiting for their next move.

When Ethan's next lengthy text came through, he relaxed a little as he read through all the instructions.

"What is it?" Claire asked.

"Ethan's found us a place to stay," he answered. "It's the home of an old client of his. He says that the place is currently sitting empty and that he's gotten the okay for us to stay there for a few nights. He says there's fresh clothes, and his client has arranged for food delivery." He hit the address and then showed her on the map. "It's a two-mile hike from here. Think you can make it?"

"For a change of fresh clothes and a promise of a hot shower, I'd walk a dozen miles," she said with a sigh.

"Yeah, I feel about the same right now. It's a good thing you don't get too attached to clothes," he said as they headed out.

"I'm not attached to them because I love shopping for new ones so much," she admitted, and he laughed.

They walked through town, avoiding as many of the tourists as they could, and headed down the water's edge until they entered a private residential area. The homes got larger and farther apart the more they walked, and he had to check his map several times to make sure they were on the correct path.

"This can't be right," Claire said, taking his hand in hers. "These places are..."

"Huge," he finished.

"Mansion doesn't come close to describing how big they are. They must be worth millions each," she said, looking around. "Someone's going to stop us," she practically whispered. "The way we look now." She glanced down at her ruined clothes.

He checked the map again and then stopped in front of a large iron gate. "This is it." There was too much greenery to see the home clearly, but he could just make out a white building nestled in the shrubbery.

He punched the code that Ethan had texted to him into the security keypad.

The gate slid open silently, and they walked through it together. They made their way up the private paved driveway as it closed behind them. The first white building was a six-car garage covered in vines. As they passed it, he could see several cars through the glass doors. There was more than one Rolls Royce, he noticed.

The paved drive turned to large pavers and narrowed into a pathway that led directly to two buildings with a courtyard in the middle. One was a three-story building on the edge of a river mouth that fed into the Tyrrhenian Sea, and the other building was a large one-story that had a green glass dome on top.

"The house." He nodded to the bigger building. "And I guess that's the pool house." He motioned to the one-story building. Through the glass windows, he could see a large pristine pool.

"Whose place is this, anyway? Did Ethan even say?"

"No." He frowned down at his phone. "He said he was going radio silent for a while and would text or call me when he could."

They made their way towards the front door. Two large pots filled with colorful plants sat on either side of the arched doorway. He used the code to enter the massive gold and iron doors.

"Oh my..." Claire dropped off as they stepped into the marbled entryway. A classical marble table sat in the middle of the area and a massive gold chandelier hung over it. They walked over to a four-story spiral staircase.

"I guess it goes down a level." He leaned over the railing and looked up and down the staircase, much like Claire was doing.

"We can't stay here," Claire said, shaking her head.

He chuckled. "Why? Too fancy for you?"

"No, it's just..." She frowned. "What if they find us again and..."—she motioned around them— "something was to happen to this beautiful place?"

"That is the point. Ethan's assured me that he was in charge of installing the security system here himself. I guarantee that the security company knew that we'd arrived the moment we stepped up to the gate. This place is just like the family's place, wired to the hilt." He motioned towards the front doors where two cameras sat overhead. "See. No one is getting close to us here." He wrapped his arms around her. "For now, we're safe."

He felt her relax as she took a deep breath and nodded. "Okay."

"Let's go find the guest room, shower, and that change of clothes we were promised. Ethan says that the kitchen was stocked, so we have food." He pulled back and looked down at her face. It was clean now, but he still remembered the trail of dried tears that had run down her dusty cheeks earlier.

She was still holding her wrist tight to her side, and he wanted a better look at it. They needed to get an ice pack on it since it appeared to be slightly swollen.

"Here, let's find you an ice pack first." He took her good hand and led her down a hallway to find the kitchen. They passed a large dining room with a wall of glass windows overlooking the water beyond. The living room, in which sat a white grand piano, had pretty much the same view. There was a smaller office decorated more femininely and then a large music room with yet another grand piano, several guitars, a drum set, and a couple stringed instruments, including a cello.

All of the floors in the home were white marble and the walls were white plaster with gold inlay wainscoting. There were expensive-looking paintings hanging everywhere under gold decorative sconces. The furniture, even though it was too dated for his taste, was no doubt worth more than his entire home.

The house was decorated in the classical Italian style and everything in the home looked expensive.

The kitchen, when they finally found it on the lower

level, was extremely modern. Compared to the rest of the house, it was a very sterile environment.

"They no doubt have a kitchen staff that comes in and cooks for them when they're home," Claire said as he looked for an ice pack in the freezer.

"Right." He gently laid the ice pack over her wrist. "How's it feeling?"

She wiggled her fingers and only winced a little. "Stiff. But the pain has lessened a little."

"Good. Maybe we can find a medicine cabinet. Shower and change first, then we can figure something out for food?"

She nodded and followed him back up the stairs. "It stands to reason that the bedrooms would be on the top floors," he said, leading her up the stairs.

They stopped on the third floor and looked in each of the four bedrooms on that level. The rooms were absolutely beautiful. Hell, they were better than any of the hotels he'd ever stayed in. But they could see personal touches in each, and he decided not to disturb the family's belongings. There had to be a guest room somewhere.

"Want to keep looking? Ethan says that we have our choice of rooms. Why not go for the gold?" He wiggled his eyebrows.

She nodded. "Let's keep looking."

They headed up to the top floor. The main bedroom was just amazing. It took up a third of the top level and looked out over both the pool house and the water. The room was personalized with pictures of a beautiful family with three kids of various races. The man was Caucasian, and his wife appeared to be Asian. There was a tall Black teenaged boy smiling over his father's shoulder, and a smaller Middle

Eastern teenage girl with her arms wrapped around the mother. The youngest child, a Black girl who appeared to be around ten, was leaning against the father. The family looked happy. Very happy. Even though the photo was obviously done in a studio, they hadn't been staged.

"Lovely family," Claire said looking at the picture, which was hung over the sofa on one of the walls.

"Yeah, they look sort of familiar, but I can't place it."

"Gavin Rogers," she said, as if she couldn't believe he didn't know. "Front man for the band No Endings?" She shook her head in disbelief.

He snapped his fingers. "Holy shit. That's right. He looks…"

"Older," she supplied, and he laughed.

"I was going to say he looks happier than he did during most interviews."

She laughed again. "It's part of the whole bad boy act he's had for years, I guess."

"Wow, this is his place?" He turned around. "Okay, we are definitely not sleeping in his bed. Out of respect."

"Agreed." She chuckled. "Let's go see what other rooms are on this floor."

There were two more bedrooms. They chose the one that looked over the green yard and the outdoor swimming pool. High arched French doors led out to a long balcony. There was a staircase that would take them down to either the outdoor pool or the indoor pool in the building just to the side.

The bathroom attached to the room was beautiful, with more white marble on both the floors and the walls. The shower had enough shower heads to blast all their aches away.

They checked the massive walk-in closets and found a

bunch of brand-new clothes hanging inside the room they had chosen. Most of the clothes still had their tags on them.

"Ethan says to help ourselves," he said, pulling out a pair of jeans and a sweatshirt for himself. Claire picked through the women's clothing and picked a pair of white cotton pants and a pink flowered shirt.

They carried the change of clothes into the bathroom and showered together.

He helped Claire shampoo her hair since her wrist was hurting her. She sat on the edge of the seat and let him rinse the shampoo from her hair.

He could tell there was something on her mind but figured she'd talk to him when she was ready. Until then, he wanted to make her as comfortable as he could.

When they were dressed in the new clothes, they headed back downstairs to the kitchen. She sat at the small table while he looked through the refrigerator and cupboards, trying to decide what to make.

In the end, the easiest was pancakes, bacon, and eggs. He knew how to cook, but after their day, he was too exhausted to do anything more.

"Want to head upstairs to eat?" he asked as he cooked.

"Honestly, I want to shove this in my mouth, then head back upstairs and shut down for a while." She rubbed her head.

"Headache?" he asked.

"Everything aches." She rubbed her hand over her heart.

"Right," he agreed as he set a plate of food in front of her.

"This is perfect." She looked down at the meal. "How is it you know exactly what I need when I need it?"

He sat beside her. To his horror, she burst into tears. Quickly, he pulled her into his arms.

"I..." she choked out. "I didn't want to do this."

"What?" he asked, running his hands through her hair as he held her.

"I don't deserve you. I'm too..." Whatever she said next came out as one long mumble as she buried her face in his chest. He did manage to hear one word, and he pulled back and looked down at her.

"You are not stupid," he said, brushing her tears away with his fingers. "I've never been in this sort of situation before, either. I don't think anyone has." She looked at him. "Honestly, if I was more into social media, I could have easily made the same mistake." He brushed his lips against hers. "I would have never even thought of it. We're so hooked up today. I mean, everything we do is watched by everyone. It's not just people we're close to following us online." He pulled her into his arms again.

"I should have thought." She held onto him. "It's my fault we're in this mess." She sighed, but thankfully she'd stopped crying.

"Yeah, I guess you should have known that buying a mask in Venice would cause all of this mess," he joked, and she playfully slapped at his arm. "I mean it." He leaned back and looked down at her with a smile. "Who buys a mask in Venice?" He rolled his eyes as she laughed and wiped her face.

"Okay, I get it," she said as her smile slipped.

"Feel better?" he asked. When she nodded, he motioned to the food. "Good, let's eat. I'm starved."

CHAPTER TWENTY-THREE

The knot in Claire's gut grew the more she avoided the topic with Justin. At some point, she needed to tell him how she felt without sounding like a complete loser. She didn't want to hurt him, but the fact was, he did deserve better. Someone who wouldn't walk blindly into danger as she had.

After eating, they were heading back upstairs when she stopped and gasped. "There's an elevator." She pointed to the thick gold doors then turned to Justin. "Seriously. An elevator." She walked over and hit the button.

Justin chuckled and stepped up beside her. "I've never seen you so excited about an elevator before."

"It's in a home," she said and realized she sounded like an idiot.

He nodded. "I can see that."

She rolled her eyes and slapped him playfully, realizing too late that she'd used her hand with the sore wrist.

"Are you okay?" he asked her as the doors slid open.

"Yeah." She swallowed the pain and stepped into the

small elevator. It wasn't the size of a normal one at a hotel, but it was large enough for at least four people.

Justin hit the button for the fourth floor, and they glided upwards smoothly.

"This is so cool," she said with a sigh.

"The band No Endings has been around since the eighties, but I didn't know they were this big," Justin said when they stepped out on the top floor.

"Gavin owns his own recording company," she said, remembering more about the man. "Hey, I think he has a recording studio here." She frowned as she looked around. "I read that it was at his place in Italy, which I assume is this place."

"It could be out in the pool house," he suggested. "We can explore that tomorrow." He took her hand and led her into the room they had chosen, which she could tell now was the main guest room.

She peeled off the clothes and climbed into the king-sized bed. She wondered how she'd ever fall asleep while the sun streamed in through the massive French doors across from them.

Justin sat on the edge of the bed beside her and fiddled around on the nightstand.

"There's..." he said just before blinds started gliding down in front of the doors, shutting out the light. "Cool. Guess that solves one question," he said when they were in total darkness. He crawled in beside her and pulled her into his arms. "Better?"

She nodded and closed her eyes tightly, willing her mind and her emotions to level.

"When we wake, you're going to have to tell me what's eating you," he said next to her ear. "Until then, I love you. I always will." He placed a kiss on her head.

"I love you too," she said, meaning it.

She woke much later from a nightmare. Her fuzzy mind couldn't remember all the details, but someone was after her, chasing her through thick fog. Moments before long fingers reached her, she woke with a start.

"Easy," Justin's soothing voice said beside her. "I've got you. Bad dream?"

She nodded as she took several deep breaths to calm her heart down. "What time is it?" she asked. Since it was so dark in the room, she couldn't tell if it was night or day.

Justin shifted and his phone light up.

"A quarter past four in the morning. Do you think you can get some more sleep?"

"I'll try. Go back to sleep." She turned in his arms and rested her head against his chest. She heard his breathing level and knew the moment he'd fallen back to sleep.

How had she grown so accustomed to being with him like this? They'd been friends forever so being around him was so easy. But it was as if they'd been stuck in a rut back home, unable to claw their way past friendship. She didn't think they would have slipped into a deeper relationship with the path they'd been going down.

She tried to think of what life would be like if they went back to the way they were before the trip, and her chest started hurting. So, she closed her eyes and willed herself back to sleep.

When she woke, the blinds were opened to the sunlight, and Justin was standing out on the balcony, talking on his phone. She detoured to the bathroom to brush her teeth with one of toothbrushes that had been left for them by the bathroom sink. She brushed her hair and tried to refresh herself as best as she could. When she stepped out onto the balcony, Justin was off the call and leaning against the railing, looking out over the water.

"Is everything alright?" she asked, leaning against his side.

"Yes." He smiled down at her. "I was just checking in. Ethan has informed our hotel and the police that we're safe and under protection. They still want to talk to us about what happened in the hotel, and it appears they've pieced together that this has happened to us many times over this trip. It will make it very difficult to stay in hiding for too long. He said that if we try to travel out of the state, our passports will be flagged."

She tensed when she remembered that her passport was still in her purse back in their hotel room. "What does that mean?"

"It means that before we can head home, we'll need to tell the police everything." He wrapped his arms around her.

It was the thing she most dreaded. She'd heard a couple horror stories about tourists getting detained by the police for some sort of misunderstanding.

"Easy, Ethan has assured me he is working on smoothing things out." He pulled her closer to his side. "How about we explore the other building and take a swim?"

"I could go for a swim."

"How is your wrist today?"

She took a moment to move it around and realized that it was much better. "Good," she answered. "Do you think they have extra swimsuits?"

He smiled. "Let's go find out." He took her hand, and they headed back to the walk-in closet.

They changed into what they found. For him it was a

pair of boxer shorts, and for her, a silver one-piece swimsuit that still had its tags on. When she noticed the price, she almost choked. But since it was the only one in the closet, she slipped it on anyway.

Then they headed downstairs in the elevator and started a pot of coffee to take with them. She washed some fruit and put it in a bowl while he toasted a couple croissants and added some jelly to a large tray he found.

They took everything with them to the outside pool area, which was on the same level as the kitchen. Here, the bottom floor of the pool house had walls of glass facing the rectangular pool, which sat on a shelf right next to the river.

They could see through the glass windows to what appeared to be a massive game room, gym, and entertainment area.

"Can you imagine having two pools?" she said with a shake of her head. "I get it, I mean, if the weather isn't nice outside, just go in." She chuckled.

"Right." He smiled at her. "Do you think they have a little bell they ring when they want drinks?" He waved his hand as if he was ringing a bell. "Jeeves, bring us some tea," he said in a hoity-toity voice.

"Gavin Rodgers does not sound like that. It would go more like...." She changed her voice and added a slight British accent. "Jeeves, bring us some tea."

Justin laughed. "You're good at that."

She shrugged. "I watched an hour-long documentary on his career last year."

"Did they mention all this?" He motioned around them.

"Not where it was located. They only showed his studio space, which..."—she glanced over at the other building—"we can assume is in there."

"Want to go explore or swim first?" he asked.

"Explore. I'm dying to see everything."

Justin nodded. "Okay." He stood up and took her hand. They left the tray with the intention of cleaning up after they had explored inside.

They stepped through the large glass doors from the outdoor pool area and explored the game room, which held a pool table, dartboards, and a bar. There was a home theater and a private gym. The furnishings in this building were far more comfortable and newer looking than those in the home across the way. This must be where the family relaxed and spent most of their time when they were there.

They found the studio at the far end of the building. It was massive and filled with high tech equipment.

"Wow, this is where it all happens," Justin said as he snapped a few photos. "My parents are going to be so jealous."

"Everyone is," she added, missing her phone but knowing she would be able to get a new one when she returned home.

There was another circular marble staircase near the two-story glass walls that overlooked the outdoor pool and water.

Up the stairs was the L shaped pool. Stone pillars surrounded the pool. Above the water was the massive glass dome, letting in the sunlight.

The wicker tables and chairs surrounding the pool matched the ones around the outside pool.

To the left was a short hallway that led to shower and changing rooms.

"This is so impressive," Justin said once they'd slipped into the water. She was floating beside him, looking up at the clouds floating beyond the glass dome.

"I know, right? I doubt any vacation I ever take will ever

match this." For a moment, she'd forgotten all the bad things that had happened to them in the past weeks.

Then Justin's hands were on her hips, pulling her close. His eyes searched hers.

"You were going to break things off, weren't you?" he said in a low tone. "Don't lie. I know you too well. I could see it in your eyes last night."

She waited a heartbeat and then nodded. "You deserve..."

"You. I deserve you," he said before he kissed her, and she knew in her heart that he was right.

CHAPTER TWENTY-FOUR

For the rest of the day, they lay around and enjoyed the pools. Both of them. She disappeared inside around lunchtime and came back with sandwiches and a bottle of wine.

He sent a text off to his parents while he soaked up some sun and assured them that he and Claire were okay. He even sent a few pictures he'd taken of the impressive place, knowing that his parents would enjoy them.

His father responded almost immediately that Ethan had contacted them and let them know what was going on. He was thankful that they hadn't been worried about them.

It was all over the news about the attack at their hotel. They confirmed that it was a concussion grenade the man had used. Thankfully, no one was injured aside from some smoke inhalation.

Just as the sun started to sink in the sky, dark clouds closed in on them from over the sea.

"It looks like rain," he said as they worked together to prepare dinner.

There was a package of freshly caught fish in the fridge,

so they'd decided to make baked salmon with a garlic butter sauce along with some roasted potatoes and asparagus.

They finished off the bottle of wine with dinner, which they had decided to eat up in the main dining room.

She'd even changed into a knee-length champagne colored silk slip dress that hugged her body perfectly. Its back was bare down to her upper back except for a few thin strings that held it up. She'd curled her hair after they'd showered off the pool water, and had found a drawer full of makeup samples, which she'd been excited over.

He couldn't remember her looking look more beautiful than she did now.

He wished there was something a little dressier in the closet for him other than a pair of jeans and a button-up dress shirt. Still, he figured it was better than nothing.

They sat in the beautiful dining room, which could easily sit more than a dozen people, with lit taper candles and soft music from the old record player in the living room and pretended for a night that this was their life.

Outside, the weather had finally arrived, and the rain pelted the glass windows. Every now and then lightning flashed and lit up the yard outside.

He was impressed at how soundproof the place was. Only the occasional boom from thunder echoed through the massive place.

He had found a container of cheesecake in the fridge along with some vanilla ice cream and wanted to surprise her with the treat.

"I'll take these dishes downstairs," he said, once they were done eating. "Why don't you sit and enjoy your wine. I'll be right back."

She nodded, then stood up. "I'm going to go sit in there." She motioned to the living room.

He took the tray of dirty dishes down the elevator and had just put them in the industrial-sized dishwasher along with the rest of their dirty dishes when the lights blinked quickly, and the power went out.

He should have thought that losing power was a possibility during the storm, but he hadn't. He thought the darkness was only a nuisance, but when Claire's scream echoed through the massive house, he rushed through the darkness towards the stairs, fear for her safety causing him to take the stairs two at a time.

Claire was enjoying the buzz from the bottle of wine and the good food. She'd been impressed when she'd spotted the beautiful silk dress that had fit her perfectly. She'd needed today. Wanted to imagine everything was normal again.

The added bonus of the beautiful location had her relaxing and enjoying herself. Justin being right there by her side helped as well.

She took her wine into the living room while he took the dishes downstairs. She sat at the grand piano and wondered how many of Gavin's songs were written right there.

She let her fingers brush the keys, wishing that she'd taken the time to learn to play a musical instrument. How nice would it be to create something... magical? Then she thought of her designs and smiled. It was her own form of art.

She was daydreaming of what she'd design when she returned home when the lights flickered and then turned off. She tensed at first, then inwardly laughed at herself for being afraid of losing electricity during a storm.

Then a bolt of lightning lit up the sky, and she saw the dark figure standing just inside the back French doors.

The man was beside her before the sound of her scream was done echoing in the large marble room. His fingers wrapped around her throat, cutting off her next scream.

"Enough," he said in a low tone as his fingers squeezed harder. "We'll just wait for..."

Just then he turned, as if hearing something. Then she heard it. Justin, running up the marble stairs, directly into danger.

She wanted to scream, to yell out a warning, but the man was cutting off her air supply. The room was so dark, she knew Justin wouldn't be able to see them.

Her hands were wrapped around the man's beefy wrists, fighting to free her airpipe. Then she remembered the piano directly in front of her.

Reaching down, she banged on the keys and watched the dark shadow that was Justin turn towards them. She banged on the keys again, only to be tossed clear of the piano. She landed on the marble floor several feet away with the horrible sound of her hip and knee banging against the hard floor.

When she recovered, she glanced up and could see Justin and the man fighting, silhouettes in front of the glass doors.

Since her throat was freed, she yelled out a warning to Justin. Told him to break free so they could run.

"Enough!" a woman's voice screamed over the grunts of the men fighting.

The larger man pinned Justin's arms to his sides.

Then the lights flashed on, and the room was illuminated in bright light. An end table was turned over and the lamp that had sat on it lay on the floor, broken.

Madison stepped forward between the two men and Claire. She was wearing a pair of black leather pants, high heeled boots, and a black leather jacket. Her long hair was in a braid down her back.

Claire didn't know what was stranger—the fact that Madison appeared to be dressed for a night club or the idea that she'd stopped to put on bright red lipstick to head out and kill. Then Claire noticed the gun in the woman's hands that was pointed directly at her chest, and she froze as she sat on the floor. The skirt to her dress was hiked up high, and she was missing one of the sandals she'd worn with the outfit.

"Well, well, the two of you have certainly moved up," Madison said with a chuckle as she looked around. "Now this is more like it." She ran her fingers on the keys of the piano.

Justin tried to pull his arms free, but the other man jerked him and tightened his hold.

"Run, Claire," Justin said, causing Madison to refocus her gun on Claire.

"Yes, Claire, do run," Madison challenged, a smile on her lips that caused every muscle in Claire's body to freeze. When Claire didn't move, Madison turned back to Justin. "Where is the list and the diamond?" she asked him, her voice turning serious.

"I have them," Justin said. "Just let Claire go and I'll get them for you."

"Oh, I think we're past the point of negotiations," Madison said smoothly. "Tell me now." She lifted the gun to aim at Claire's head. "You have until the count of ten." She smiled as she started counting down from ten.

"They're upstairs," Justin yelled before she said nine.

"I'll take you to them. Just... don't," he said, sounding totally defeated.

Justin's eyes searched hers, and she saw what she'd wanted to deny. There was no more hope. They'd run out of luck.

"I'll take you to them," she said as tears burned her eyes. Whatever happened now, she wanted to give Justin as much time as she could.

"Go," Madison waved her gun towards the stairs. Then she turned to the man holding Justin. "Rubio, if I don't return in five minutes, kill him." Then she added, "Slowly."

Claire got up from the floor, kicked off the other sandal, and walked towards the stairs. Madison moved behind her and nudged her forward with the butt of the gun in the middle of her back. The cold steel caused shivers over her naked skin.

"At least you're finally wearing something that's not tacky," she said. She laughed when they reached the first landing. "Oh, cheer up, Claire. At least you'll die wearing Armani." She chuckled.

Claire stopped at the base of the stairs, her feet unwilling to move when Madison's words sank in. It took a shove from the gun in her back to get her to move again. "Where?" Madison asked.

"Up," she said, her throat completely dry.

The gun nudged her forward to the next step.

"How'd you find us?" she asked. Fear of her messing this up for Justin played in her head again.

Madison chuckled. "We tracked Justin's phone."

Claire stopped in the middle of the staircase. "What?" she asked, glancing over her shoulder.

"He left it sitting on the table at the wedding. It was a good thing I had the contingency plan to install the location service and share his information with my phone when he wasn't looking." She chuckled. "I think he was dancing with you at the time. The two of you looked so in love on the dance floor." She nudged the gun in her back again, and Claire started walking. "I should have checked after I hit the two of you, but I assumed and, well, you know what assuming does." She chuckled as they reached the top of the stairs. "Where?" she asked again.

Claire started heading towards the bedroom just as a large crash sounded below them. A gun went off below them and Claire cried out.

Her eyes were filled with tears at the thought of losing Justin. Madison leaned over the balcony's edge and called down, "Damn it, Rubio, I told you to wait five minutes."

In that moment, Claire's tears dried, and her fear turned into rage. Without thinking, she rushed towards Madison and shoved as hard as she could.

The sound of the woman's scream as she fell over the marble balcony would never leave Claire's mind for as long as she lived. She watched Madison's arms and legs flailing, reaching for any hold as she fell the four stories before landing with a dull thud on the hard marble floor below. Instantly, blood pooled around her body as her empty eyes stared up at Claire.

Then she heard another shot, and Justin screamed her name. As he'd done before, she darted down the stairs, her bare feet barely making a sound as she rushed towards danger. The only thing in her mind and heart was Justin.

When she ran into the living room, Justin was lying on the floor next to a very dead Rubio as a large man in all black stood over him, holding a gun.

Without thinking, Claire picked up the nearest thing

and tossed it at the man's head. The crystal vase skimmed the man's temple and sent him falling forward.

"Claire!" Justin said quickly. "Stop. This is Ethan." He stood up and rushed towards her and wrapped his arms around her. "You're safe," he said into her hair.

"Ethan?" Her eyes went to the man who was now bleeding from a cut on his temple. Ethan chuckled as his hand came away from the cut covered in blood.

"Yup. It's nice to meet you too," he joked. "Sorry I'm late to the party."

Justin held Claire's hand as they stepped into A Taste of Italy together. Seeing the crowd of people holding signs and cheering for them warmed his heart and made Claire laugh.

"Guess we have a hero's welcome," she said right before she was engulfed in hugs from her father and sister. Then his parents were there, holding onto him as well.

Shortly after the incident at Gavin Roger's place, Ethan had decoded the CDS drive. On it was a complete copy of Carmine Stefani's kill list. Those that the ruthless mob boss had killed in the past and those he currently had hits out on to keep his organization in power.

The official news out of Italy was that famous heiress Madison Hayes had taken her own life by jumping off a balcony at her family's villa while on vacation in Venice.

Rubio's death was ruled as a car accident when his body was found in a mangled stolen Rolls Royce just outside of Rome. No one cared enough about the death of some unknown mobster to look into why there were the two bullet holes in the man's chest.

There were more than a hundred people crowded into the restaurant to welcome them home. For the party, his father had set up a buffet table since the staff were part of the celebration.

When the karaoke machine started up, he pulled Claire up on stage and picked the song "Stand by Me," remembering how she'd sung it in the hotel shower.

She laughed as he started signing it and when the first chorus came, he took her hand and knelt down on one knee and sang clearly.

"So darlin,' darlin,' marry me, Oh, marry me, Oh, marry, marry me."

Claire's eyes widened and then teared up. Then she was laughing and pulling him to his feet and hugging him as the crowd around them cheered. The music was shut off as everyone demanded Claire's answer.

"Yes," she said loudly as she laughed. And then she kissed him as he spun her around to more cheers.

The West Series

Loving Lauren

Taming Alex

Holding Haley

Missy's Moment

Breaking Travis

Roping Ryan

Wild Bride

Corey's Catch

Tessa's Turn

Saving Trace

Christmas Holly

The Grayton Series

Last Resort

Someday Beach

Rip Current

In Too Deep

Swept Away

High Tide

Sunset Dreams

Lucky Series

Unlucky In Love

Sweet Resolve

Best of Luck

A Little Luck

Christmas Wish

Silver Cove Series

Silver Lining

French Kiss

Happy Accident

Hidden Charm

A Silver Cove Christmas

Sweet Surrender

Second Chances

Entangled Series – Paranormal Romance

The Awakening

The Beckoning

The Ascension

The Presence

The Calling

The Chosen

Haven, Montana Series

Closer to You

Never Let Go

Holding On

Coming Home

The Hard Way

Pride Oregon Series

A Dash of Love

My Kind of Love

Season of Love

Tis the Season

Dare to Love

Where I Belong

Because of Love

A Thing Called Love

First Comes Love

Someone to Love

Wildflowers Series

Summer Nights

Summer Heat

Summer Secrets

Summer Fling

Summer's End

Summer's Wish

Distracted Series

Wake Me

Tame Me

Stand Alone Books

Twisted Rock

Hope Harbor

Raven Falls

Angel Bluff

For a complete list of books:

http://JillSanders.com

ABOUT THE AUTHOR

Jill Sanders is a New York Times, USA Today, and international bestselling author of Sweet Contemporary Romance, Romantic Suspense, Western Romance, and Paranormal Romance novels. With over 75 books in eleven series, translations into several different languages, and audiobooks there's plenty to choose from. Look for Jill's bestselling stories wherever romance books are sold or visit her at jillsanders.com

Jill comes from a large family with six siblings, including an identical twin. She was raised in the Pacific Northwest and later relocated to Colorado for college and a successful IT career before discovering her talent for writing sweet and sexy page-turners. After Colorado, she decided to move south, living in Texas and now making her home along the Emerald Coast of Florida. You will find that the settings of several of her series are inspired by her time spent living in these areas. She has two sons and off-set the testosterone in her house by adopting three furry little ladies that provide her company while she's locked in her writing cave. She enjoys heading to the beach, hiking, swimming, wine-tasting, and pickleball with her husband, and of course writing. If you have read any of her books, you may also notice that there is a love of food, especially sweets! She has been blamed for a few added pounds by her assistant, editor, and fans... donuts or pie anyone?

facebook.com/JillSandersBooks

twitter.com/JillMSanders

amazon.com/Jill-Sanders/e/B009M2NFD6?tag=jillm-com-20

bookbub.com/authors/jill-sanders

instagram.com/jillsandersauthor

www.ingramcontent.com/pod-product-compliance
Lightning Source LLC
Chambersburg PA
CBHW031011190726
48286CB00003BA/796